THE E

The

By

Margaret Brazear

Copyright © Margaret Brazear 2015

CHAPTER ONE

"You look beautiful, my love," Michael said with a wistful smile.

He bit back the quiver which touched his lips. Seeing his little sister standing there in his wife's pale blue wedding gown, little sapphires glittering all over the skirt and the sleeves, took him back to the day he had stood in the church and watched Christine slowly walking towards him.

That had been the happiest day of his life, although he did not know it then. He had no idea why his sister was so insistent upon wearing the gown, and he had tried to talk her out of it, but in truth he could refuse her nothing. She was very fond of Christine and Michael thought she wanted to wear the gown because she would not be here to see her wed. He thought it was so Grace could feel closer to her. He was wrong.

The first time he saw Christine was at the coronation of the new Queen, and at the banquet afterwards he found it difficult to take his eyes off her.

It was not just her beauty which attracted him; there were many beautiful women there, all richly dressed and sophisticated, yet Christine's natural beauty set her apart. Her blonde hair fell about her shoulders in waves and curls, not twisted into impossible shapes by some clever hair stylist. Her skin had its own sheen, free of powder or potions to obscure its natural glow. And he watched her every move, the gentle way she touched her father's arm as he sat beside her, the soft laughter when something amused her, the shine in her bright blue eyes as she watched the new Queen presiding over the feast.

The several parts of her gown were of a combination of pink satin and white lace. Her bodice was quilted satin, pulled tight so that her high bosom swelled and bounced gently as she moved. Her overskirt was pink satin and her petticoat was of gleaming white lace. Her sleeves were the same pink satin, but quilted and interspersed with pearls and she wore a necklace of matching pearls.

Her hair reflected the light from the candles overhead and Michael longed to discover how her lips would taste.

In Michael's opinion, she outshone the new Queen, who was a pretty young girl, too young to be occupying the throne of England, but hopefully she would marry soon and seek guidance from a foreign Protestant prince.

Elizabeth had red hair, like her father, and her gown was impossibly heavy, with layer upon layer of elaborate brocade, stitched with many copies of the Tudor rose and trimmed with ermine. Her bright hair hung loosely down her back, as befitted a maiden lady, and the crown perched on her head was solid gold with many rubies glittering in the candlelight.

After the five year violence of Queen Mary's reign, all the people here were hoping for great things from this Queen, young as she was.

But she could not compete with the lovely young girl who had caught Michael's attention. He had to know who she was, had to know if she was someone he was entitled to pursue.

Occasionally she looked his way and smiled, the most glorious smile he had ever seen. Her even teeth were white, her lips smooth and her blue eyes kind. He felt sure she had sensed him watching her, and he blushed, glanced away, but not before that smile had captured his heart.

When he asked about her, the disappointment almost brought him to tears.

"She is Lady Christine," the steward told him. "The daughter of the Duke of Westerbury."

The daughter of a duke! Oh, no! He tried not to look at her again, but it was too late; he was enchanted. He was but the second son of an earl, important though that earl might be. He was not even the heir to his father's title and estate; his elder brother held that privilege. She was the daughter of an important duke and a lady in her own right; he could offer her nothing. His Grace would intend her for an earl at the very least, possibly the heir to a duchy; certainly a viscount of small fortune, with no prospect of climbing higher would never do.

All four brothers, along with their father, were in high spirits. The Queen's claim to the throne was easily challenged, but the people had cheered her enthusiastically along the route of the procession the day before and on her way to Westminster Abbey today for the coronation. They were as sick of the brutal reign of her sister, Mary as the Melfords and they had come out in their thousands, despite the cold January weather, to show their approval and sniff the fresh, clean air to be sure the stench of burning flesh had left no residue to linger over the city.

There were a lot of noblemen who still wanted a Catholic monarch, despite the brutality of Queen Mary's five year reign of terror. There would always be those who wanted things their own way, especially where religion was concerned. As to that, Michael and his brothers were not pious in any religion and were quite happy to go along with what was safest.

The fact that Elizabeth had not attended her own coronation mass, held in Latin, and had retreated whilst the holy communion was performed, told them all that this may well be the last Catholic mass.

***

Michael stayed away from court circles after that. He had no wish to meet Lady Christine again, not when his ambitions toward her were so hopeless. The following months crept by slowly, as he tried his best to put her out of his mind, to look to other maidens as a possible Viscountess for him. But his dreams would not comply with his wishes; he often woke from a deep sleep thinking Christine was his after all. He had even reached out for her in the night, only to awake with a start and feel the disappointment all over again.

And those dreams always brought with them a stab of jealousy which was alien to Michael. He was of a placid disposition and had never been jealous of anyone or anything in his life before. He had no real idea of the meaning of the word, but now he knew, now he was very jealous of whoever would be chosen to be husband to Lady Christine.

As the months went by, he knew she would not stay free for long, that even should she not have been married, she would definitely have been promised. What manner of man would be fortunate enough to win her hand? And would he feel for her as Michael felt for her? Would he appreciate the treasure he had won, or would he think merely of her riches and lands, her status in the world? Michael often woke to find his hands clenched into fists, ready to do battle with whatever man had won the love of his life.

It was foolish; he had not even spoken to her. How could he be in love with her? She could be a spiteful, envious sort of female for all her knew. But he could never believe that. Anyone with that smile, with eyes as kind as hers, had to be perfect and perfection did not come along twice in a lifetime.

He tried hard to focus his interests in other directions. He nagged his father about building a new house, one in the shape of an E, as was the fashion since Elizabeth Tudor took the throne. Melford Manor, in which the family had lived for generations, was badly in need of modernisation as well as major renovations.

There was plenty of land going spare, but the old Earl would have none of it; he did not like change. Michael had little hope of his brother ever building such a house when he inherited; Malcolm was not averse to change, but he was very much averse to spending money.

Michael also had his eye on a beautiful black stallion, 17 hands and a wonderful beast, but his father was in control of the money and he would not spend that much on an animal. To the old Earl, a horse was no more than a convenient form of transport and one such mount was as good as the next. His only requirement in such a creature was that it was healthy and strong and fitted its rider.

Michael realised all these plans which occupied his thoughts were mostly to suppress his real desire, and no amount of money would buy her for him.

He had begun to think he would remain unmarried, that no woman could ever come close to meaning to him what Christine had come to mean to him, when the unthinkable happened. It was a family tragedy which should have left him devastated, but instead filled his heart with hope. He had always felt guilty about that, but it was out of his control and there was no help for it.

Both his father, the Earl of Melford, and his elder brother, Malcolm, were killed when their carriage was swept down a hillside during a gale. Suddenly Michael was the powerful and wealthy Earl of Melford himself and in a position to petition for the hand of Lady Christine in marriage.

Wealthy people were building houses in the shape of an E in honour of the new Queen and Michael was suddenly in a position to do the same. So much power was very intoxicating; his first action was to send word to the owner of the stallion, telling him he would be prepared to buy the creature. Then he sent word to a well known architect to design his new house.

Both these deeds could be accomplished within minutes, while he was dressing with care for his visit to the Duke of Westerbury and his most important acquisition.

He could not even wait a decent period after the double funeral to race to the Duke's estate some ten miles away from Melford Hall in Essex. He had to get there before it was too late, if it were not already too late, and he mounted his late brother's horse, which was faster and fitter than his own, in order to get there as quickly as possible.

His stomach fluttered throughout the journey as he turned over in his mind the best way to ask for Lady Christine, and what he would do if the Duke refused, or if he was too late and she was already promised to another man.

The latter would be worse. He could do his best to persuade the Duke, but if she was promised elsewhere it would be much harder.

She was barely fifteen but by the standards of her class, she should have been promised years ago. Why had Michael not considered that before? Why had he not realised? He had no idea, but still he was determined to try. His success depended on who he had to compete with. Betrothals had been broken before.

When he arrived at the Duke's country mansion he saw her, walking in the formal gardens with a young man. Michael recognised him at once; Edmund Carstairs, the younger son of a minor baron whom he had met at the occasional local function.

Michael sat on his horse and watched the couple for a few moments, trying to judge how friendly they were with each other. He noted that they did not touch, that she did not hold his arm or even walk close to him. Good; at least he seemed to be only an acquaintance.

Carstairs was not at the palace for the coronation nor for the banquet afterwards; his family were not important and were unlikely to have been invited.

Again that treacherous surge of jealousy rose up, but he forced it down. Christine would not be promised to this man; if he thought for one moment he had kept quiet because of his low status while she had been betrothed to a man of less importance, he would never forgive himself.

He could not believe his good fortune when the duke agreed to his proposal.

"As you may know, Your Grace," he began nervously, "I have recently inherited the Melford title and estates on the sudden death of my father and brother."

The Duke shook his head slowly, his mouth turned down.

"I have heard, My Lord," he replied. "You have my condolences."

"Thank you. I hope you will not think me impetuous, or acting in bad taste to take advantage of the situation so soon after the event. Their deaths have left me in a position of holding the title and the wealth, but of having no bride. I was hoping to speak to you about your daughter."

His Grace raised one eyebrow.

"My daughter?"

"The Lady Christine? I have no idea what her situation is, or what you might have arranged for her future, but I hope you will look favourably upon my petition for her hand in marriage?"

A smile escaped the Duke's mouth, quickly forced away but not before Michael saw it. His hopes soared; it seemed the Duke did look favourably upon the request.

"My Lord," he replied. "I am very pleased to hear your petition. The fact is my daughter has been keeping company with young Edmund Carstairs, a nice enough young man, I suppose, but the youngest son of a northern baron. He can offer her nothing, in addition to which his family are Catholic. I will not be sad to have a good reason to part them."

It never occurred to Michael that Christine might have a preference for Carstairs; she was very young and in his opinion not old enough to know her own mind or heart.

He had inherited everything which would have gone to Malcolm, but he had no intention of inheriting his brother's betrothed. She was not to his taste; he found her manner dour, she was far too thin and he never did understand how Malcolm could be so content to wed her. One night in his cups he had let slip that he had no intention of giving up his mistress for her and that he was marrying her only for her lands which adjoined Melford lands. He intended to stay with her only long enough to sire an heir.

Michael said nothing to his brother at the time, but that was not the sort of marriage he wanted for himself. What happened to Geraldine when Malcolm was killed, he had never enquired. She was sent back to her father along with her dowry and he never gave her another thought until now.

Comparing her with Lady Christine, comparing the swell of that lady's bosom over the satin bodice with the almost flat chest of Lady Geraldine, almost made him laugh.

No, he had not thought about Christine's wishes; all he knew was that he wanted her. He wanted to stroke that smooth skin, wanted to run his fingers through those lovely tresses, wanted to slip that bodice from her shoulders and hold her silken body against his own.

Did he even ask if she felt the same, if she wanted him? No, he did not. He had made the mistake of assuming she would be grateful for an illustrious title and wealthy husband. He was handsome enough and generous; he thought he could make her fall in love with him.

He was wrong.

***

That had been three years ago and now, watching his sister in his wife's wedding gown, with that same fair hair cascading over her shoulders, he could almost believe it was Christine, back in his home again.

"Thank you, Michael," Grace said, her expression grave. "I want to look my best for the Viscount you have told me I am to marry."

Michael sighed impatiently. He thought they had finished with these discussions, but apparently he was wrong.

"You told me you liked him," he said. "We have discussed this many times; you have had every opportunity to decide whether you would suit each other and you told me you were happy with the match. It could cause no end of problems to break the betrothal now; such an act could ruin your future, you know that."

Michael had gone to a lot of effort to find a man who would suit his sister. After the collapse of his own marriage, for which he blamed himself for his lack of respect for Christine's wishes, it was very important to him that Grace was happy with this marriage.

"Oh, it has nothing to do with liking him," she said with a mischievous little smile. "I like him very much; he is handsome, personable and very charming. I am grateful for all your efforts on my behalf, Michael, really I am."

"Well then?"

Grace paused, her lips twisting into a little thoughtful pout, before she replied.

"I will not marry him unless My Lady Christine is there to see it."

He stared at her. Their mother died giving birth to her and Christine had been the only mother she had ever known, albeit only briefly. She was almost as heartbroken as Michael when Christine left him, so why was he surprised at this turn of events?

She had done this on purpose, he was sure of it. She had made no mention of this before, had waited until it was too late to change things without scandal. This was the reason behind her insistence on wearing his wife's wedding gown, when she could have had her own newly made one; she wanted him to see her in it and remember his own marriage.

He tried to keep the anger out of his voice, but was not very successful.

"Grace, you know that is impossible."

"I know no such thing," she replied with a little pout. "I do like Viscount Jason. Given time, I might even learn to love him, just as you love your wife."

"That is all in the past."

"Is it? Then why does her portrait still hang above the hearth in the great hall? Why does her likeness still look down on you in your bed?" She gave him a stubborn look. "I would have thought you might have put those images away in the attics, or even destroyed them altogether, were Christine really in the past."

"Grace, you are being unreasonable. She left us; you know that."

"Again, I know no such thing. She may have left you; I cannot know the truth of that as you have never shared it with me, but I know she would never have left me, not without a word of goodbye, and she certainly would never have left her baby daughter. You should have known that much, if nothing else."

Grace stepped down from the stool where she had been standing for the dressmaker to finish her hem and allowed the woman to remove the gown. She stood in her shift and petticoats studying her brother, and he knew she was hoping for the right response to her demand.

She had made these same arguments before, but always Michael had swept them away, afraid to remember the rift between him and his wife and he had always ended by telling his sister she was too young to understand. Now she was to be a bride herself, he could hardly use her age as an excuse.

Her words resounded in his brain, made him catch his breath. She was right; Christine would not have left little Lisa. The child was not even a year old and Christine adored her; was it likely she would leave that baby girl for a man? And why the hell had Michael never even considered it before? Could it be because he was so blinded by jealousy he thought only of himself, just as he had thought only of himself when he asked for Christine in the first place?

"You are going to marry Jason," he told Grace. "There is no choice now, not for you."

She laughed. He knew why she laughed, because she knew very well he would give her anything within his power. He might threaten to be the heavy handed guardian, but in truth she was always able to manipulate him as easily as Christine could.

He often wished he had stopped his wife from leaving, from going to the man she had wanted before her father forced her into a marriage with Michael. But when he saw them together, it hurt too much and he was consumed by a rage he had never felt in his life before. He allowed his jealousy to get in the way.

He had walked into her bedchamber in this very house and seen them, kissing. Edmund Carstairs was holding Michael's wife in his arms, pressing her lips against his, her breasts against his chest as he kissed her passionately and Michael's heart twisted then as it twisted now to remember it. She pushed Carstairs away when she saw him there, but not before he had decided in his fury that she was not worth fighting for.

"I knew it!" He shouted. "I knew you would never be able to give him up!"

"Michael, please," she begged as she took a step toward him. "It is not what it looks like."

He heard no more; he marched out of the chamber as quickly as he could and although he knew she called after him, he had put too much distance between them to hear what she said. He was desperate to get away from them both. Tears were welling and he needed to hide those tears from this treacherous pair.

"Go!" He shouted back at her. "He is welcome to my leftovers. Whore!"

Michael returned to London and his little daughter and tried to calm himself. But he got no rest; he missed Christine so much, he ached for her. His dreams found her beside him in his bed, her sweet lips on his chest, her soft arms wrapped around him.

It was a week or so later that he returned to Essex; he could stand it no longer, and thinking about her sharing herself with that man produced in him an unfamiliar and murderous rage. Nothing had ever hurt him as much as losing Christine and if there was a way back for them, he wanted to find it.

He felt a fool for even thinking of forgiving her, told himself it was for the sake of their child, but when he arrived at Melford Hall it was to find she had gone.

It was early spring and not yet time for the household to return from London, so only a pair of caretakers visited the house once a day.

Christine had left their London house early, had come here to his country estate because, she said, she had promised one of the tenants she would be godmother to her new baby.

Now he realised that was only a ruse and her real reason for coming to Essex had been to meet with her lover. He suspected that, which was why he followed her. He wanted to come with her, but she said there was no need, that she would be gone but two nights. Two nights spent in his house with Carstairs!

Michael had never been able to trust her, not since shortly after their marriage when Carstairs appeared at Melford Hall in pursuit of his lost love.

The man hung about outside, probably waiting for an opportunity to see Christine alone, but Michael was not going to allow that. He crept up behind him, not wanting to give him a chance to flee.

"What do you want here?" He demanded.

Carstairs drew a deep breath.

"I have come to see Christine."

"Lady Christine to you," Michael snapped angrily. "What do you want with my wife?"

"I want to talk to her, to be sure you are treating her well."

"How dare you?"

"I dare because you stole her from me. She was mine! She is still mine in her heart and always will be. Did you even ask her if she wanted to marry you? Did you?"

Michael was silent. No, he had not asked her. He had asked her father for her but never once had he asked her. The Duke had said she was keeping company with this man, but Michael had thought nothing of it. He had never even considered that she might be in love with him.

"You know as well as I do," Michael replied, "that His Grace would never have allowed a marriage between you."

"That does not answer my question, My Lord. She loved me before you came along and ruined everything. You do not simply turn off your feelings; she loves me still and always will."

"Get off my land!" Michael yelled at him.

But he had always had his doubts, ever since that day. Even then he did not ask Christine if Carstairs spoke the truth. Why had he not asked? Because he feared the answer, but the man's words ate away at him and that was not the only time he heard them. Carstairs returned after the birth of their daughter, rousing Michael's jealousy and insecurity even more, until the day he followed her from London and found her in his arms.

He had his suspicions; he would not admit that at the time, but it was true. He wanted to trust her, he wanted to show her that he trusted her by allowing her to go to Essex without him, but he let his fear of losing her decide for him.

He arrived at his country house just a few hours after her and saw the strange horse tied to a post outside. Jealousy flared and twisted him into some sort of monster he did not recognise and when he ran up the stairs and marched into her bedchamber, saw her in the arms of another man, he fled before his rage took him too far.

He could have killed the man, easily, but he never wanted to hurt her. She was still the love of his life, even if her heart did belong to another.

When he returned, the house was deserted as it always was at that time of year. Villagers came in once a day to keep the dust from accumulating, but that was all. The full staff were with the family in London.

He clung to the hope that he might be wrong. He mounted his horse and rode to the village, to the woman who had wanted Christine as godmother to her baby. There was a small gathering in the cottage, where the woman had only recently given birth, and the priest was there, ready to take the child to the village church. But there was no sign of Christine and Michael's heart sank.

"Has Lady Christine been here?" He asked, feeling foolish.

The new mother sat up in her bed and shook her head.

"No, My Lord," she replied. "She did promise to be here, but she never came."

He asked no more questions, just mounted his horse and rode away. He could scarcely believe that Christine had disappointed that simple woman, it was so unlike her, but he supposed it was her only chance to escape with Carstairs.

He questioned the few cleaners who were in the house, but they had seen nothing, except Carstairs' carriage driving away.

In Christine's bedchamber he searched her clothes chests, found some of her clothing gone, but not all. Michael had lavished many fine garments on his wife, as he always wanted to see her in the best his inheritance could buy and it was difficult for him to know how much was gone and how much remained.

The sapphire necklace he had bought her when they married was still there, in her jewellery chest. In fact, she had taken none of her jewellery; Michael assumed she felt some flicker of shame which prevented her from taking jewels her husband had bought for her. But her ring was gone, presumably still on her finger where he had placed it on their wedding day.

There was little point in continuing with the search. It seemed to him she had taken enough clothes for but a few days, but he could not be sure. She had a lot of clothes, a lot of fine garments, and all of them seemed to be here in her chests. Perhaps her lover would replace the ones she had left behind. His mouth turned down in a bitter grimace as he left the house.

That had been almost six months ago and now he stood and gazed at the portrait above the fireplace, his Christine with her beautiful, thick fair hair, with that same pale blue satin gown his sister would wear for her own wedding. He did not want her to wear it; he thought it would hurt too much to see her in it, but he had said nothing. Why spoil her day because he had failed to make his wife happy? That is what he had thought when she made her request; now he suspected Grace had an ulterior motive.

As he stood and studied that sweet face, his sister's words forced their way into his memory. *She certainly would never have left her baby daughter.* Why had he not considered that before? He was driven by jealousy, had believed then that her desire for another man was her priority and she knew her child would be safer with her father. That had to be the reason; he had thought he knew her well, but seeing her in the arms of that man made him realise he knew nothing about her, nothing at all. And his jealousy consumed him, made him wild with fury until he could think of nothing but the pain he wanted to inflict on Edmund Carstairs.

He had made no further attempt to find her. He loved her enough to want her happiness, no matter the cost to him, and if she was in love with another man, he wanted her to be with that man. It made him look weak, he knew that, but he cared nothing for appearances, only for Christine and her happiness.

Now he suspected Grace of wanting to wear Christine's wedding gown intentionally to remind her brother of what he had lost, to force him to bring his wife back whether she wanted to come or not. And if she did not want to come, did he really want her? The answer was yes, even if she never spoke to him again, at least she would be here with him, where he could look at her if nothing else, where he could drink in her beauty and live on dreams of what might have been.

His sister was devious, knew how to slowly and patiently contrive a situation in order to get her own way, and he now believed this was it. Why else would she insist on wearing a three year old gown when she could have the finest fabrics and the best dressmakers to make her a new one? She must have known all along the affect her appearance would have on him. She had even curled her hair to resemble Christine's.

He was angry, but more angry with himself for not realising before this what she was up to. He was also a little amused and impressed by the way Grace had managed to manipulate him.

He retreated to his bedchamber and lie down on his back, staring up at the embroidered velvet canopy above his bed as he remembered when he first saw Christine and tried to decide the best way to find her and persuade her to return, if only for that one day.

CHAPTER TWO

Grace sat behind the yew hedge in the newly landscaped gardens, enjoying the afternoon sunshine. The garden was beautiful, but it had taken a long time to grow how her brother wanted it and too late to present to his wife, for whom it was cultivated. Still, he would have his second wish; it was finished in time for his sister's wedding. He had even had the gardeners grow a maze like the one at Hampton Court, although Grace rarely ventured inside it, and never alone. She hated the helpless feeling she got in there, as though she was not in control.

She felt a little of that lack of control now, as she wondered if her brother would grant her wish and bring his wife home for the wedding. She wanted to force his hand, as she knew he had made a horrendous mistake by letting her go. Grace had not been given enough facts to know precisely what happened in the spring, but she was quite sure Christine would not have gone without saying goodbye. Something was not right about the whole situation and she needed him to see that.

She wanted Christine here; she missed her, missed their time together when they would talk, when Grace would tell her about her fears and dreams. Christine was the only one she felt able to talk to about intimate things. She could not talk to her brothers and although she loved Helen, she did not like her submissive attitude to her husband. Grace did not think she would understand, not like Christine understood. And she was helpless to do anything about it. Her plan to wear the wedding gown and remind Michael of what he had thrown away might be cruel, but it was necessary; she had hardly seen him smile since Christine went away, and she would give almost anything to see that warm smile again.

The house was built in the fashion of grand country houses, in the shape of an E in honour of Queen Elizabeth. The land upon which it was built had been a meadow, part of the original Melford estate and mostly used for grazing horses. Michael had paid a lot to have the house finished in time for his own wedding, and even then it was still lacking a few carvings.

The estate stretched for miles, all the way down to the sea, and although Grace had lived here all her life, there were parts of it she had never visited. She had never been allowed on the cliff side of the beach, as her father, and later Michael had deemed it too dangerous. Nobody ever went there; it would take only a strong wind for someone to be swept off the edge and out to sea. Further down the cliff were the remains of a small fishing village which the sea and wind had destroyed, if proof were needed that it was not a safe place. There was but one cottage left high on the cliff and it got closer to the edge every year as the land eroded and the sea moved closer.

Grace and her brothers were all born in the old Manor House and raised there, but when her brother inherited the estate, he decided to build his own house, a place to bring his bride on their wedding day.

The old house still stood in the distance; her father had presided over that manor, with its white walls and thatched roof. But Lord Michael wanted his own, new house to go with the earldom he never expected to inherit. The intention was for her brother, James and his wife to live there when it was renovated, but for some unknown reason they still lived in the new house, which Michael had called Melford Hall.

The Manor House would never be demolished. It held far too many fond memories; they had all been born there, even their father, and their mother had died there, giving life to her only daughter. Grace still felt a little guilty about that, despite being told over and over that it was not her doing. Had Michael had his way, she would never have been told how her mother died, but her father had his own way and his way was to always speak the truth, no matter how much it might hurt. She would have loved to have known her mother though, would have given almost anything to have her at the wedding.

Her eldest brother, Malcolm, died along with his father when their coach overturned in a storm and tumbled down the side of a steep hill. Fate took a hand that day, fate decided it wanted Michael to have the earldom, wanted Lady Christine for its countess.

But the marriage had not lasted and Grace wanted to know why. She loved Christine, had loved her since the day Michael brought her home as his bride. Despite Grace's rank and her rich clothing and her nurses, Christine had recognised that she was still a little girl in need of a mother and she had become that mother. Grace did not believe she would have left her or her own baby Lisa, and she felt she was entitled to know the truth.

Everything Grace knew about life, about marriage and the duties of a wife, about the joy of love and motherhood, she had learned from Christine. She it was who had made her anticipate her own wedding day with pleasure instead of fear and she was determined to have her here to witness that pleasure.

She heard a footfall beside her and looked up, startled out of her thoughts.

"Forgive me, My Lady. I did not mean to approach so stealthily."

Her gaze swept over Viscount Jason, the young man she was to marry. It was not appropriate for them to meet alone like this, but Grace was not of a temperament to concern herself with such conventions. Indeed, she was glad of the opportunity to speak to him alone before it was really too late. Despite her brother's warnings of scandal, the betrothal could be broken, although not easily. She privately thought the custom of tying oneself for life to someone you knew nothing about to be very bizarre; it had done her brother no good, certainly.

"It is perfectly all right, My Lord," she replied. "Come and sit beside me."

He looked around, frowning at their surroundings as though concerned about something.

"If you would not mind, My Lady," he said, "I would much prefer we go somewhere else."

"How so? Are you afraid to be alone with me?"

He turned his head towards the centre of the lawn before he answered, smiling at her jest.

"There is a bench over there, with nothing beside it but a rose bush which will hide nobody."

"You are afraid of being overheard?"

He nodded, and to her delight, held out his hand. She took it in her own, felt the warmth from his smooth skin and smiled. When they reached the bench and sat together, he kept hold of her hand, a gesture she found comforting.

"I wanted an opportunity to speak with you alone," he said. "All the arrangements and the expense, and nobody has asked either one of us how we feel."

She turned her face to him as a sudden thought struck her.

"Oh," she said. "Do you object? You do not want to marry me?"

"No, please…"

"Because if that is the case, I wish you would say so. I do not think I want to be tied to a man who has a fancy for another maid."

He was shaking his head as she spoke.

"No, no," he said. "Nothing like that, not at all. I shall be honoured to have you as my wife and in time, my countess. You are very beautiful and you seem to have a gentle disposition."

"As do you, My Lord, but appearances can be deceptive."

"That is very true."

"What did you want to say to me?"

He took a moment to gather his thoughts before he answered.

"I want to be sure you want this marriage," he said. "Like you, I have no wish to tie myself to someone who does not want me."

She smiled, touched by his concern and pleased he had noticed her reticence. It spoke to his perceptive nature, a trait she had always thought her brother should have more of. If he had, he might not have lost the woman he loved.

She reached up a hand to Jason's face, kept it there long enough for him to turn his head and kiss her palm and felt a shiver deep inside before she quickly removed her hand.

"It is nothing to do with us, with you and me," she said. "You may or may not know that my brother's wife disappeared some months ago."

"I knew the Earl and his wife had parted."

"More than that. My brother says she left us, but I have never believed that."

"Why not?"

"Because she loved him," she said. "Whether he could see it or not, she loved him and whatever problems they may have had between them, I do not accept that she would have left me or her baby." She turned to stare at him defiantly. "Does that sound conceited?"

"Not at all."

"She was a good mother. She was always a good mother, to me and to her own little daughter."

"Perhaps things changed," he said soothingly. "You cannot know what goes on between a man and his wife. They would likely have wanted to keep the truth from you."

"Perhaps," she said. "But I still do not believe she would have left me or Lisa."

"Is this what has been making you sad?"

She nodded.

"I have told my brother I will not marry unless she is there to see it." She turned to look at him, touched his face again. "I am sorry, Jason."

Grace thought he might be angry, but instead he nodded thoughtfully and she was surprised when he slipped his arm around her shoulders and pulled her toward him.

"Then we must find her," he said after a moment. "And we do not have much time."

CHAPTER THREE

James, Viscount West, brother of Michael was now the next in line for the title should anything happen to Michael, who had not stayed with his wife long enough to father a son.

Thinking of that made him angry. The couple had produced a daughter, so the woman was quite obviously capable of giving birth to a healthy child. It would have been only a matter of time before a son came along, but Michael had to be noble and let her run off with her lover! What the hell was he thinking?

James would never have let his wife go; indeed she would never have been allowed the freedom to meet with a former suitor and put him in that position. He knew why Michael had done it – because he was besotted with her and wanted to give her what she wanted, even if what she wanted was another man. Michael felt guilty for having married her the way he had, the way earls often did.

Had Michael been the firstborn son, a maiden from a noble family would have been sent to live within their household, just as Geraldine had been sent to eventually marry Malcolm. But as a younger son, things had been more lax and the accident which killed the old Earl and his heir had left Michael in the position of having the title and estate, but no bride.

James recalled the months between Queen Elizabeth's coronation and the fatal accident, when Michael would not stop extolling the virtues of Lady Christine. He had become boring on the subject, every word out of his mouth was about the woman. It became so nobody could get him off the subject. Michael had not so much as exchanged a word with her, but still he thought himself in love.

He had pointed her out to James at Westminster Hall, and he could certainly see the attraction; she was very lovely, and very sweet looking. Obviously not as sweet and innocent as she had appeared.

He had lost no time in asking for her. To marry as he had, by arranging things with her father and not getting to know her, not even meeting her, was not unusual, but Michael had to feel guilty about it.

James shook his head dismissively; now he would one day inherit and although he was quite happy with the prospect, he loved his brother and thought him a fool for not stopping his wife from leaving with that man. He should have brought her home before it was too late, before she was completely ruined and by force if necessary. It was too late now; she was sullied, unfit to bear the heir to Michael's title and estate.

If he had found his wife in the arms of a lover, he would have killed him and dragged her back where she belonged, not let her go off with him because it was what she wanted.

The only way for Michael to father a legitimate heir now would be to divorce his adulterous wife and marry a more virtuous woman. That could take years, but James could see no other way; if only he could persuade Michael of that.

His own wife had been faithful, had given him two healthy children, both sons, and although he had never told her so, he loved her well enough. But not enough to let her go to another man; that he would never tolerate. Apart from anything else, it would make him look a complete fool, just as Michael looked a complete fool to his peers as well as his underlings. That fact also infuriated James.

He sat at the window drinking wine from a silver goblet and gazing out at the formal gardens which had cost his brother a small fortune. From up here, he could see every pattern formed by the shrubs, the yew hedges and flower beds, and it did look magnificent. James knew Michael had wanted the gardens for Christine and that alone made him think them too expensive.

Now he watched his sister, sitting with her betrothed. He frowned disapprovingly. They should not be sitting there unchaperoned, even though the betrothal was already settled, but at least they were in full view. He would keep an eye on them, make sure nothing untoward happened.

He saw Grace reach up a hand to the young Viscount's face, saw that young man turn his head to kiss her palm and was half on his feet, ready to intervene, when she moved away. He was still undecided as to whether he should go down and separate the couple, when the door opened after a brief tap on the oak and his brother entered.

When their father and elder brother died, guardianship of their young sister naturally passed to Michael as the new Earl, but James thought he would have made a much better job of it. Next thing they knew, Michael would be letting Grace run off and do as she pleased, just as he had his wife. No doubt the young couple were sitting alone with Michael's blessing.

Now he glanced up as Michael entered.

"Just in time," James said. "I have been observing our sister and her betrothed, being rather too familiar with each other."

Michael strode toward his brother and leaned over his chair to peer out of the window. He smiled.

"You are such a misery sometimes, James," he said. "How can you find anything wrong in two people who are to be married sitting together and talking."

"That rather depends on what they are talking about, I would have thought," he answered. "Just now they were holding hands, and she was caressing his cheek."

"Really? How wonderful!"

James sighed.

"You are far too lenient, brother," he said. "Little wonder your wife left you."

He knew he had gone too far as soon as the words left his mouth and he saw his brother's angry scowl.

"Forgive me," he said hastily. "That was callous and really none of my business."

He was genuinely sorry. He had his own ideas of how Christine should be dealt with, but he could see that his words had hurt Michael and that he never wanted.

"No, it is none of your business," Michael answered. "Nevertheless I have come for advice on that very subject."

James gave him a frown of curiosity.

"My advice? You do surprise me."

He was remembering the quarrel they had had when Christine first ran off with Carstairs, when Michael had returned to London without her and told him what had happened.

James had been horrified and privately Michael had gone down in his estimation, although he would never have told him that. The feeling did not last long, at any rate, but at the time he had been furious. He had advised his brother to bring her home and lock her up until she learned her place. He even said something about giving her a good beating, which suggestion resulted in him finding himself on the wrong end of Michael's fist.

"I do not wish to hear any of your barbaric ideas, James. I wish to know how I should proceed. Grace is saying she will not marry the Viscount unless my wife is present."

James laughed, tossed back the remainder of his wine and stood to pour more, along with a second goblet for his brother.

"Were I her guardian, she would not be so sure of herself as to refuse," he said.

"I knew you would say something like that, but that is not the advice I need. I need to know how you would go about finding Christine."

James looked at him thoughtfully, his mouth twisting as though wondering whether to reply tactfully or truthfully. He decided on the latter.

"You have decided to bring her home after all? Despite her having been defiled by another man for more than half a year? You missed the chance to stop that, to stop him getting his hands on her, to stop her playing the whore for him. I think, brother, it is too late."

"I want her to come back to see our sister married. She was like a mother to Grace and I want her to have her at the wedding if that is what she wants; whether Christine will want to stay is not something I have even considered."

"Ah, but you will take her back if she does, will you not? You are besotted with her."

"James, be reasonable for once in your life, please. Supposing it was your wife."

"It would not be my wife," he answered, raising his voice to an angry shout. "Helen would never have been allowed the freedom to betray me in the first place."

Michael slammed down the half full goblet and turned to the door.

"I should have known better than to apply to you for help," he said. "I wonder if you have ever asked yourself if Helen is happy with her lack of freedom. I wonder if you even care."

James watched his brother leave the room, slamming the heavy oak door behind him. He did not want to admit that his words had jolted him, but what he said was true. He never had thought about Helen's feelings, whether she was content to be the wife he had made her. She was an intelligent woman; he allowed her to read her books and even to write her poems as long as she did not try to publish them, but he did like her to consult him before she did anything out of her normal routine.

He it was who decided on the education and conduct of his two sons, but he saw nothing wrong with that. He always assumed that when they had a daughter, Helen would have her own say in such things.

It was not as though he accompanied her everywhere she went. Once a month, she travelled the few miles to her father's estate to visit him; since her mother died when she was a child, he imagined the old man looked forward to seeing his only daughter. He never accompanied Helen on these visits, but in truth he did not get on with her father and would rather not have to listen to his illogical raving. The old man was still Catholic, had support Queen Mary in her efforts to restore England to the Church of Rome, even approved of her violent methods to achieve her goal. The man would not stay off the subject, either, and James could barely be civil to him.

The dressmaker who was designing Grace's wedding clothes would be back this afternoon and James planned to ask her to make new gowns for Helen. He thought she would be pleased with the gift, but he realised now he was doing it for his own gratification, not for Helen at all. Always, when new clothes were ordered for her, he was present to choose the colours and the fabrics. He remembered Christine once telling him with disgust that her father did that, watched every stitch the seamstress placed in every fabric and style he had chosen.

He scoffed; why was he considering the words of a trollop? His attentiveness to Helen's clothing was nothing to do with wanting to control her wardrobe, more to show an interest in her and what she did. He would be failing in his duty to her if he showed no awareness, would he not?

As it turned out, he was glad to be there when she had chosen that awful yellow silk last season. He was thankful to have been able to tell her how sallow it would make her look.

He filled another goblet with wine; this was one more than he would usually consume at this time of day, but his brother had unsettled him. Perhaps he should show his wife more affection, perhaps he should give her leave to decide some things for herself. But, damn it! That course led to the sort of heartache Michael had been suffering for most of this year. That path led to nothing but trouble.

He glanced out to see if the young couple still sat together, but they were gone. Instead he saw Michael pacing about the garden and his conscience pricked. His brother asked his advice, which must have hurt his pride, and the only response James was able to give was condemnation. He needed to remedy the situation.

***

Michael wondered why he had expected to get any real sense or advice out of James. They did not think alike, that had been made clear when Michael returned to his London house last spring without Christine. James had berated him then, told him he was a fool, and while he actually agreed with him, he could not bear the thought of forcing his wife to live with him against her will. He loved her too much for that; he did not want to see her unhappy, he did not want to go to her bed each night knowing he would be forcing himself on her. And he was certain he would never recover from the rejection he was bound to face.

Only now did he think about that and realise she had never behaved as though she did not want him. He had been so hurt and so determined to give her what she wanted, it had never occurred to him before.

Now his memory showed him their wedding night, after the feasting and dancing, when he had taken her hand and led her to her bedchamber. He gave orders that the guests were not to be allowed to accompany them and as they left the hall, he sensed the crowd trying to follow, turned to see his servants blocking their way.

This was to be the first time they had spoken together, the first time they had been alone and he was not about to share it with anyone. Even the priest had been told he was not needed. Blessing the marriage bed was a relic of a superstitious age as far as Michael was concerned, but now he wondered if his refusal to allow the ritual was to blame for the failure of his marriage. He shook himself sternly; what rubbish! He was the only one to blame for the collapse of their marriage, he who should never have married her in the first place.

But now he had his doubts even about that as he paced about the gardens. These gardens were beautiful, fashioned on the ones at Hampton Court, and he had ordered them planted and cultivated for Christine. Just looking at them hurt; she had never had the chance to see how beautiful they would look in the summer, as they looked now.

He had held her hand all the way to the bed that night, stood and watched as one of the maids unlaced her bodice and removed her wedding gown, the same gown his sister was to wear for her own wedding.

He had been pleased with himself, as pleased as he was when he saw the almost finished house he had commissioned, or when he collected the very expensive stallion he had been hankering after. She was his latest possession, his newest purchase; he realised that now. If only he had realised it at the time.

Thinking back, remembering that night, he recalled Christine had looked nervous. She flushed crimson, which he had taken as maidenly modesty. He now realised it was embarrassment that this stranger stood and watched her clothing being removed as though she were some tavern dancer and he a leering spectator.

He had not leered, had he? His heart sank; he hoped not. That would be crass and not how he wanted to welcome her as his wife.

His thoughts returned to his brother and James' opinion of how women should be treated, and he realised with a dart of shame that he was no better. He had been thinking of Christine as a possession, as something he had bought and paid for and wanted to make use of.

When the maidservant had gone, leaving Michael's new bride in her silk shift, he had taken her in his arms and kissed her. She had returned the kiss, he was certain she had, and when he undressed and they stood together beside the bed, she had not been unwelcoming. She was nervous, of course she was, what else would a man expect?

"I want to please you, My Lord," she said shakily. "But I have no idea what you expect of me."

He had smiled, delighted to find her so naïve, so innocent. Only now did he wonder if she was trying to tell him how she really felt.

"There is nothing to fear," he said. "I will be gentle; I will not hurt you, I promise."

He wanted her there and then, felt his body responding to her beauty, but he did not want to frighten her with his ardour. He slipped her shift from her shoulders and let it fall to the floor, swept his eyes over her naked body and the urge to cup her breast was irresistible. He swept her up in his arms and lifted her onto the bed, began to stroke her gently, kissed her breasts, her neck, her lips and waited until she panted, breathless, before he entered her. She gasped and tremored then and he knew he had broken his promise.

"Forgive me."

She clung to him, ran her hands over his back, pulled him closer.

"It is better now," she whispered.

He had pleased her, he knew he had. She had lain beside him afterwards, her head resting on his chest and her arm around his waist. He even recalled how she had brushed her lips over his nipple and caressed him, wrapped her arms around him. Would she have done that, treated him with such tenderness, if her affections lay elsewhere?

"Are you all right?" He asked her. "I did not hurt you, did I?"

"Only a little. It will be better next time."

Her words were encouraging; at least he had not frightened her.

"Tell me something, Christine," he said. "Why were you free to accept my proposal? I wondered why you had not been promised to another long ago."

She laughed gently; he felt the vibration of her laughter in a little flutter against his chest.

"Nobody was good enough," she told him. "My father turned away many gentlemen and their sons; I think he was hoping for a Duke or at least the heir to one, but no such person came forward. He was getting desperate, running out of options."

He frowned at her, turning his head to see her mischievous grin, then he laughed, realising he was meeting her sense of humour for the first time.

"I do not believe that," he said.

"Well, it is partly true. He promised my mother on her deathbed that he would not see me married before my sixteenth birthday. That being the case, other suitors had decided they did not want to wait."

"Fools."

"You have Edmund Carstairs to thank for his early acceptance, My Lord."

He had been stroking her shoulder, his fingertips moving in little circles around her flesh; her words stilled those fingers. He suddenly remembered what the Duke had told him about Christine keeping company with Carstairs; he had not given him a thought before.

The mention of his name here on their wedding night, after such intense and glorious lovemaking, produced a swell of jealousy and anger he had never felt before.

"What has he to do with it?" He demanded.

She failed to answer straight away and he knew he had frightened her. He did not want that.

"He kept coming to the house to see me, just as a friend. But Father did not like it, thought there was more to it. That is why he decided to hurry the wedding; that is why he was pleased when you asked for my hand."

Had she told him Carstairs was just a friend because he had become angry? Were her words designed to appease him?

"Just as a friend? Are you sure about that?"

She sat up, holding the covers over her naked breasts while she turned her head to look at him. He could see she was a little afraid; he was angry and she knew nothing about him. She must have been concerned with what form his anger might take, whether he was likely to channel that anger into violence.

When she spoke, her voice quivered and her cheeks flared crimson.

"Are you calling me a liar, My Lord?"

His eyes met hers and he regretted how he must have sounded, how he must have scared her. He reached up a hand and stroked his fingers down her naked back.

"Forgive me," he said. "I should not have questioned you. It was unfair and uncalled for."

She lie back down and rested her head once more on his chest, while he hugged her closer, angry now with himself for frightening her. He was certain he was in love with her and he wanted more than anything to make her love him back; scaring her was not the way to do it.

He wondered what had come over him. He was not given to losing his temper, but he had never known what jealousy was before and he hoped never to feel it again. Alas, his hope was to be disappointed.

The festivities went on for the rest of the week and each night Michael made love to his bride, and each night was a little better than the first time. They rose together to heights of passion he had never known before and he was sure she returned his passion, that it was not pretence.

It was when the guests had all left that Edmund Carstairs showed his face the first time, told him his wife had been in love with him, that Michael had stolen her away against her will. He had let the man's words fester, let them fuel his jealousy.

She welcomed him into her bed each night until she discovered herself with child. She must have conceived on the first night, or at least sometime during that first week, which meant he had to curb his passions. But he remained faithful to her; he did not go and find a mistress to give him comfort as many men in his position did. He was always proud of that; he was also proud that he had welcomed their first born, despite the baby being a girl.

James seemed to be more disappointed than Michael.

"It is good the babe is healthy," he said. "You can only hope it will be a son next time."

He did not even congratulate Michael on the birth of his firstborn; it was a disappointment. He had a healthy son, his wife was expecting another and James believed his brother should be disappointed. Once more, he thought him weak.

"I suppose you think a woman has some control over the gender of her child," Michael said.

James shook his head, but still frowned with disapproval.

"Of course not, Michael. That would be silly, but I do think your wife should be made aware that she has let you down."

Not for the first time, Michael wondered if he could persuade James to take his family and move into the old manor house, even though the renovations were as yet unfinished. How they lived under the same roof without bloodshed he could not fathom.

Michael had built this house for himself and his wife, and James had brought his wife and baby to stay here, along with their younger brother, while the manor house was renovated. Grace naturally lived with him as he was her guardian. They had never seemed in any hurry to leave. Michael had made his house too comfortable, that was the problem.

"She has not let me down, James," he answered wearily. "She has given me a beautiful daughter and I am grateful."

He was, too, and he could not wait to return to her bed and take her to himself again. It was but a week before the doctors deemed it safe, when he saw Edmund Carstairs again.

He saw him as he rode out to check on some fences that had come down. He wanted to be sure everything was as it should be in the village and with the scattered cottages of the tenant farmers. He was a generous landlord and always approachable, although he had yet to convince them of that. They thought he was like his father, who had held himself aloof from the ordinary people and took little interest in their welfare.

Edmund Carstairs seemed to be trying to hide, watching and waiting for Michael to leave the house, to be far away before he approached. Michael rode his horse to stand beside him and stared down at him from his great height.

Once more that jealousy threatened to consume him and he felt his fingers tighten over the hilt of his whip, almost of their own volition.

"What are you doing here?" He demanded.

Edmund looked up at him, his expression implacable, but made no reply.

"Well?" Michael said again, his voice rising. "Why are you loitering about my land?"

"I have come to see Christine," he replied.

"Lady Christine to you; I told you that before, or Lady Melford, if only to remind you that she is my wife. What do you want with her?"

"I want to see her, to talk to her. What are you afraid of?"

"Not you, Sir, that is certain. I will ask her if she wishes to see you. If she does, you may come up to the house."

Was that too reasonable? Michael asked himself as he turned his horse and made his way back to the house. James would never have allowed a meeting, but he was not James. His only hope as he went in search of Christine was that she would refuse to see her visitor.

"I will see him, Michael," she said. "But only to assure him of my happiness, only to tell him to go away, to leave me alone."

"Then I will invite him into the house, but I will stay with you, if you do not mind."

She stiffened, drew herself up.

"That is your choice, My Lord," she said with a note of displeasure he could not fail to notice. "You are my husband; if you do not trust me to be alone with Edmund, that is of course, your decision."

Once more he had made a mistake, once more he had said the wrong thing.

"Forgive me," he said. "Of course I trust you. But I do not like the man and I fear for your safety."

She almost laughed, would have laughed had he not looked so grave, he was sure of it.

"He is no threat, Michael," she answered. She stepped toward him and stood on tiptoe to kiss his cheek. "He is infatuated, nothing more."

"And you? Are you infatuated?"

Then she did laugh.

"I am, I think, yes." She paused just long enough for him to capture his anger and get it under control. "But not with Edmund. I am very much infatuated with my husband."

"Really?"

She stepped into his arms and reached up, her lips met his and the passion in her kiss could not be denied, yet still the jealousy burned within him.

He waited in the next room during their meeting, the door slightly ajar so he could hear. He hoped Christine would never know it, but the need to hear what she would say was overpowering.

He should have been relieved and joyous to hear her tell her visitor she loved her husband, was happy in her marriage and ask him not to return. Why could he not trust her words?

When at last Carstairs came out, he stood to face him.

"She does not mean it, you know," he told Michael.

"What are you talking about?"

"Christine. She knows you are out here, listening. That is why she told me she had no love for me. It is a lie; perhaps she is afraid of you. She will not speak the truth while you are within earshot."

"How dare you?"

"If you hurt her, I will kill you."

Michael could contain his rage no longer. He still held that riding whip and now he raised it above Carstairs head and brought it down, striking his face.

"Get out!" He shouted. "Get out of my house and never show your face here again!"

Edmund left, clutching his injured cheek, and Michael felt his wife's touch on his arm.

"Do not listen to him, Michael, please," she said. Tenderly, she rested her head on his arm, kissed it through his shirt. "I love you. You do believe me, do you not?"

He heart sang. She said she loved him and he desperately wanted to believe her, but Carstairs' suggestion that she feared him resounded in his mind. He remembered how he had frightened her on their wedding night, and could not get that image out of his thoughts. Was she afraid? Is that why she told him she loved him?

He wanted more than anything to believe her, but he could not dampen this awful jealousy, could not suppress the rage which came with it.

Now he sat on the stone bench in the gardens, the bench recently vacated by his sister and her Viscount. He had gone to a lot of effort to be sure he chose well for Grace, had insisted on waiting until she was older before agreeing to a betrothal. He was afraid she would not love him, that he would not love her and he never wanted her to know the heartache he suffered.

He heard a footstep and glanced up to see James approaching; he scowled. He was still angry with him, with his attitude. He should pity him really; he would never know what it was to really love as Michael loved Christine.

James sat beside him, folded his arms.

"I am sorry, Michael," he said. "I know you loved Christine, I know you did what you thought was best for her. I will never understand it, but I know why you did it. Now you want to bring her home to witness our sister's marriage, but have you really thought about it?"

"What does that mean?"

"It means have you considered what affect it will have on you, seeing her again? I remember the state she left you in; I do not want to see you go through that again. You must realise that if she comes back, it will be for the wedding only. Are you prepared to let her go a second time? It is too late to make her stay; she is not fit to be your wife, not now."

Michael's jaw clenched and he turned angry eyes on James. He did not want to argue again, but if his brother did not stop insulting his wife, he would not be able to keep himself from hitting him.

The two brothers often quarrelled as they did not agree on very much, but they had always been friends. The only time they had come to blows was over Christine and that only made James even angrier with her, Michael knew.

"I have thought of none of those things, James. I thought only of making Grace happy, of granting her wish while she is still our little sister, before she becomes somebody's wife."

"That is half your trouble; you are too concerned with making others happy. You forget yourself."

"Is there another way to treat those one loves?"

James stared at the ground thoughtfully, as though looking for the courage to voice his thoughts.

"If you are so concerned with Christine's happiness," he said, "why have you never divorced her so she can marry Carstairs?"

"What?"

"You heard me. If you divorced her, she would be free to marry her lover but you have not done so. Why?"

"Divorce would cause too much scandal; she would be outcast. It would take years of arguments, our private lives would be exposed for everyone to scrutinise, to shake their heads over. I could not do that to her, or to me, or to Grace, not to mention my daughter."

"Are you sure it is not because you hope one day she might return?"

"What if it is?"

"Michael, she is a whore." He watched his brother's jaw clench angrily, watched his hands bunch into fists and remembered being on the receiving end of those fists, but still he went on. "You can hit me again if you want, but it is true and you know it. She has been living in sin with Carstairs all these months, she is sullied by him, yet you would still take her back. You would still want to go where he has been; I cannot understand it."

"No, and you never will, because you know nothing of love. Helen has my sympathy."

He got to his feet and marched back toward the house, wondering once again why he ever imagined he would get any useful advice from James.

CHAPTER FOUR

In the twelfth century, King Henry II had four sons, the youngest of whom was nicknamed John Lackland because, out of all of them, he had nothing. His father had vast dominions, England, Aquitaine, Normandy and more, but with three elder brothers, there was nothing left for John.

The youngest son of the late Earl of Melford gave himself a similar nickname – he was also called John and he, too had no lands. Often the youngest son would take holy orders, become a monk or a priest, but John had avoided that fate. His father had tried to force the issue and his death had come as a relief to his youngest son; at least now he would not have to run away and become a mercenary or some such, as his brother was far more understanding of his wishes.

Malcolm would have agreed with his father and John might have still had a battle. He had no real belief in God; there had been too much bloodshed in His name over the previous centuries for John to believe, but he dared not tell that to his father.

Now things were different. Michael was a man who liked to make up his own mind about things and he saw no reason why others should not have the same privilege, even women. He had allowed his wife more freedom than any man John had ever known, but such leniency had resulted in his own destruction.

Being the youngest, John was privy to information about his brothers only when he eavesdropped on their many arguments and for the first time in his life, he found himself agreeing with James. Michael was far too lenient, but it was his own decision and not for anyone to interfere. He just thought it a pity that he would spend his life alone, because the only woman he could ever love had left him. Michael would not even seek out a woman for hire or take a mistress; his marriage vows still meant something to him, despite them meaning little or nothing to his wife.

But John had thought little about his brother's situation. He had his own worries, his own concerns. Michael and James might have stepped up the ladder with Malcolm's death, but John was still the youngest son with no land and no money. He had to find a way to survive, preferably in the style he had been accustomed to.

Perhaps if Michael did not have his head full of Christine he would find his youngest brother a wealthy wife, as he saw no other way to ever be his own man.

For now he helped all he could for his keep. He oversaw the estate, the tenants and the village, made sure the bailiffs were doing their jobs, became an intermediary between the underlings and the Earl. They took their concerns to John, as they found him less intimidating than James and Michael was the Lord, someone they did not always feel comfortable in speaking to, despite Michael's easy going nature. That had been their father's doing; he always thought himself too important to mingle with the tenants and villagers. Michael would never have kept up that particular tradition, if he were not so distracted by his own heartache.

This morning he had overheard his little sister telling Michael she would refuse to marry Viscount Jason unless Christine were there to see it. John had been listening outside the room where the dressmakers were making alterations to Christine's wedding gown. He wanted to know what affect it would have on his brother, seeing Grace in that gown, so he listened and what he heard made his heart leap in his chest.

She was demanding that Michael find Christine and bring her home for her wedding, and that demand changed everything. For John kept a secret which weighed heavily on his young shoulders.

If everything had gone to plan, or at least the half formed plan John had made, he would have been long gone from Melford before this. At the beginning of spring, he had decided he was growing weary of being John Lackland and owing everything to Michael's generosity. He decided he needed to leave, to make his fortune in the world one way or another.

He was not yet twenty and lacked not only wealth and lands, but a bride. Nobody wanted to betroth their daughter to a penniless, younger son with no prospects. But he was an adventurous soul. He envisioned leaving Melford; he imagined himself crossing the channel to France, exploring that country even though none of it now belonged to the English crown. Queen Elizabeth's half-sister and predecessor had seen to that, when she lost the last of England's holdings in France.

Or he could go to Scotland, perhaps find friends among the Scots. Neither country were friends of the English, but that could change and often did. Young John had many ideas, each one thrilling him with an excited tremor, until the day he came here to Melford Hall at Michael's request, while the rest of the family stayed in London.

Michael wanted him to check the fences and the animals after the winter storms. He had bailiffs and stewards for that sort of thing and while he trusted them, he recognised that the safety of the estate was ultimately the responsibility of its Lord. He had assigned John the task of overseeing things, but John suspected it was merely to give him something to do, to make him feel he was earning his keep.

He had been to the main house, had told the servants to prepare the house for the return of the family in the next few weeks, then ridden to the Manor House to be sure the builders were finished and it was fit for James and his family to occupy.

John would move back there with them, he supposed, although the new hall was much bigger. In truth, he would rather live in Michael's house than James', as he was always closer to his older brother, but it was really up to Michael. He would have to wait and see how the land lie when the family arrived back in Essex.

When he had finished with the duties Michael had asked of him, he decided to ride towards the sea; he always found watching the waves helped him to think, and he had much about which to think.

He rode to the very edge of the Melford estate, to the part which was never used even for sheep grazing, the part which overlooked the beach and which was gradually eroding with the harsh winter weather.

There was a solitary cottage there, right on the edge of the cliff and overlooking the sea. It was abandoned, had not been used within John's memory, likely because of its position. It got really windy up here in the winter, so windy that there was a danger of livestock being swept over the cliff to perish on the rocks below.

If the meadows were dangerous, so too must the cottage be. John had no idea why it was there or who it had been intended for, but he thought it likely to have been a fisherman and his family. He vaguely remembered hearing that Melford once had a small fishing village, and further down the cliff there were the remains of a few cottages which had not survived the last bad flood.

The village had been abandoned many years before when John's grandfather had built new dwellings for the fishermen in a safer place. John could see the tumbled bricks; it was obvious the whole village had been swept away along with the cliffside itself. The remaining cottage must have been further back before that, in a safer position.

It was a warm day and there was a definite feeling of spring in the air. The birds were singing and that fresh smell filled his senses and gave him hope for the future. But it was chilly up here in the wind. John did not know how this one solitary cottage had survived, but it obviously had and that day he approached it out of curiosity, just to see if anything was left worth salvaging. He was surprised to see movement behind its open shutters.

It was bigger than the dwellings in the Melford village, and seemed to be made out of wattle and daub with a thatched roof. The roof was surprisingly intact, almost as though someone had recently patched it up, but John could not see how that could have happened.

He sat in his saddle and watched the cottage for some time, hoping for the occupant to show himself, but nothing happened so he dismounted and left his horse standing. The animal would not bolt, not with this lovely lush grass to munch on, and John walked toward the cottage stealthily so as not to startle whoever was inside.

He was expecting to find some vagabond or beggar who had found the cottage and claimed it as his own. Michael would not disapprove of that; he believed everyone should have the basic needs of just being human, but John thought he would want to find a safer place for whoever it was. This place was all right now, as it would be through the summer months, but once the autumn arrived, followed by a harsh winter, it might not survive.

Whoever was in there failed to notice him as he continued to approach stealthily. He knew that sometimes these people were treated harshly by overlords and bailiffs and he did not want him to bolt before he had a chance to offer him shelter.

What he saw when he finally reached the open door and peered inside convinced him that he was asleep and dreaming. The blonde hair, the pretty, childlike face could not be mistaken. She wore a cloak of red wool, a peasant's cloak, and she was leaning over a fire, poking the cold ashes with a stick.

He caught his breath, half convinced he must be imagining things. She could not be here; she was living with Edmund Carstairs, had been for weeks, probably at Carstairs Manor or one of the other houses belonging to the man's father. Carstairs was fairly well off, if not titled, and this woman was living with him. She had left John's brother a heartbroken wreck to live with him, so why was he seeing her apparition in this place? Was she dead? Was he seeing a phantom? And why would her ghost find shelter in this desolate hovel?

"Christine," he murmured almost to himself.

She spun around, startled by the strange voice, and stared at him. He stepped toward her but she took a step back, pulling her cloak closer around herself. Her eyes were as wide as a startled rabbit and for one awful moment, he feared for her sanity. This was not the confident woman he had learned to love as his brother's wife.

A treacherous little voice rose up in his mind, a little voice which spitefully muttered: *serves her right*. He shook his head to push the little voice away.

"It is me," he said soothingly. "John. Do you not recognise me?"

"I do. What do you want?"

"What do I want? I want to know what you are doing here."

He paused and looked about the rough whitewashed walls, the sandy rushes on the dirt floor. It was fairly spacious as these cottages went; it had two rooms, this one and another beyond a roughly made wooden door, and it had a fireplace and chimney, much like the ones at the main house. That was an unusual addition. There was a spit fitted over the cold fire with a cooking pot hanging down from it.

He turned back to Christine.

"Why are you living like this, Christine?" He asked. "Michael believes you to be living with Edmund Carstairs." He dropped his voice to what he supposed was a sympathetic tone. "Did it not work out as you hoped?"

Her eyes filled with sudden tears and she stepped quickly toward him, gripped his jacket in her bunched fists and looked up at him pleadingly.

"Please, John," she said. "Do not tell him I am here. Tell no one, I beg of you."

"Why not? He will be concerned for your safety. He will want you to come home; Michael would never allow you to live like this."

"Perhaps not," she said. "But I do not want him to know I am here."

That is when he felt the little flutter from beneath her cloak as her stomach brushed against him. He held her at arm's length and looked down at her slightly swollen figure, realised at once why she wanted her whereabouts to remain a secret.

A surge of anger rose up inside him. How dare she come back here, carrying another man's child? This place was not fit for a countess and Michael would never forgive him if he left her here, but he did not want his brother to know about this.

"Very well; if that is really how you want it," he said. "How long have you been here?"

"Since Easter," she answered.

Easter? It was at Easter that she ran away with Carstairs. How could she have been here all that time? He did not understand, but he did not feel benevolent enough towards her to ask. If she had suffered at the hands of her lover, so much the better. She would realise what manner of man she had turned her back on.

John had no idea what to say, how to handle the situation. Christine, daughter of a duke, Countess of Melford, was living in this rough place, open to the elements and the harsh weather, and she was with child. Michael would want to know she was here, but would he want to know about the baby? He decided not; his brother had been hurt enough, he had no need to know about his wife's condition.

"I shall keep your secret, for now, but I will not leave you here. The Manor House stands empty; I will get the keys and take you there."

"No, he might find me there."

"Michael? Why are you afraid of Michael? You must know he would die before he hurt you, no matter what you have done."

"I am not. I am afraid of Edmund. That is why I was hiding here, so he would not find me."

John's heart melted and he drew her close and kissed her forehead.

"What did he do to you?"

She shook her head.

"It is not important, not now. Nothing is important now except this child and my little daughter. Is she well? Does she miss me?"

"She is well, yes. You need have no fear on that score. As to whether she misses you, perhaps you should have considered that before you decided to satisfy your lust at her expense."

She stepped away from him and raised her hand a little; he thought she was going to slap him and he would not have blamed her. His words were harsh and he had no right to voice them.

Once more her eyes filled with tears and she turned away; once more his heart melted. He would not get far as a mercenary if he could not even lay blame where it belonged.

"The builders have finished with the Manor House. It has not been decided if James will return there straight away. There are two villagers who go there once a week to dust the place and make sure all is well. Apart from that, nobody ever goes there. The place is full of priest's holes, left over from King Edward's time. They will make it easy for you to hide; I will show you."

"Priest's holes?" She said. "But your family are Protestant."

"Yes, they are, but my mother was not. She kept a priest in the house to say mass for her."

The shadow of a smile touched her lips.

"Your father must have loved her very much to allow that."

"He did. He was more like Michael than he cared to admit."

The bitterness in his voice was unmistakable, but Christine made no comment. Why should she explain herself to him, after all? He was just the younger brother, the one who took care of the menial tasks nobody else wanted to do just so he could feel he was not a wastrel.

"I will be back with the keys as soon as possible," John said. "At least you will be warm and comfortable there, if nothing else."

"And you will not tell Michael?"

"No," he said, shaking his head. "I will not tell Michael. Were it not for that," he nodded toward her swollen stomach, "I would. But he has no need of further heartache."

"If you really mean that, you will give me funds to hire a midwife," she said.

His eyes swept her figure and he grimaced. He could not leave now, could he? He could not go to Scotland or France, or the Americas to seek his fortune. He had a duty to his brother, to keep him from more heartache by caring for this woman.

"I will try," he said. "How long?"

"It should come in the early autumn," she replied. "I still have a little time."

John left, feeling her gaze following him as he mounted his horse and rode slowly toward Melford Hall. His thoughts were racing; it was after the Easter festival that Christine had left; he vaguely recalled an argument. She had been here, for some reason, not with the rest of the family in London. After the celebrations and the service in Westminster Abbey, she had left London and he seemed to recall something about her promising to be godmother to one of the tenants when she gave birth.

Michael, in his usual way, allowed her to come down here alone. That was what the argument had been about, John thought now as he rode slowly back to Melford Hall. It had not been between Michael and his wife, had it? It had been James, interfering as usual, who Michael was arguing with. James told him he was a fool to let her come down here alone, that she was likely meeting Carstairs.

Michael had told James all about Edmund Carstairs. Despite their difference, they shared their most private concerns and John knew because they never really noticed whether he was there or not. Michael had always worried about that man, hanging about, trying to tempt Christine away.

She had taken the carriage and returned to their country house and because of James' insinuations, Michael decided to follow her, found her with Carstairs, found them together in her bedchamber and it had been too much for him to forgive this time. He had left her there, returned to London and never saw her again.

Now she was here and with child. John felt a great weight burdening his young shoulders, felt his plans for the future shattered, as he asked himself what the hell he should do.

***

As Christine watched Michael's young brother riding away, his words echoed through her mind and she felt betrayed all over again, just as she did when Michael called her a whore and left her to her fate. Of course John believed what Michael had told him, that she had come here before the family to meet with her lover. Everyone would believe it, not just the family, but the villagers and tenants as well, the servants and everyone else would think her a whore.

She remembered that day, remembered it as clearly as though it were yesterday. She had nightmares about that day, awoke with her face wet with tears and an ache in her throat which threatened to choke her.

She had enjoyed Christmas, her daughter's first, had loved entertaining important families with Michael at her side. She had really enjoyed giving special gifts to all the servants and presiding over their special Christmas feast.

Michael had given her a lovely white fur cloak as a gift and their nights were as passionate as ever. She loved him and she knew he loved her. She thought herself so fortunate, especially when she observed the way James and Helen were. Sometimes she felt she could shake her for her submissive way of treating her husband, but it was none of her business and Helen seemed to adore him.

She had no real wish to leave the family, but she had a duty. She came to stand as godmother to one of the tenants; she had come because the woman's baby was due and she had promised.

She had been here but a few hours, changed her clothes and got herself ready to visit and see if the birth had yet begun, when Edmund appeared. She had not locked the door; she did not see the need.

"What are you doing here?" She demanded.

"I have been waiting for you to come," he answered. "I have been sleeping in the barn, just waiting for the day you would come back here and I could tell you I am wealthy now."

She only stared at him, not sure what she should say. That was before she knew he was insane, when she still thought he was her friend.

"How so?" She asked.

"My father died at Christmas, then Roger succumbed to food poisoning. Everything belongs to me now."

"Well, you have my sympathies. To lose them both so close together must have been hard."

That was when he took a step toward her and gripped her arms.

"Do you not see?" He said excitedly. "This means we can be together."

Christine pulled away, her heart beginning to hammer fearfully.

"Edmund, I am married to Michael. We can never be together."

"He is not important," he replied. "I know you loved me. You cannot simply switch off your love because he came and stole you away."

She backed away, feeling afraid of him for the first time in her life and that was when they heard the footsteps on the staircase, that was when they heard Michael's voice calling her name.

She was so relieved, she almost collapsed. Had Edmund not appeared, she might have been angry with Michael for following her here, for not trusting her, but instead she was so thankful he had come to save her. But as the door opened, before she could form the words to tell her husband what was happening, Edmund pulled her into his arms and kissed her. She struggled, but he was a powerful man and she was trapped in his embrace, unable to move, much less get away.

And Michael called her a whore, told Edmund he was welcome to his leftovers. She managed to push away her captor, as Michael turned toward the stairs, and she called out to him.

"Michael!" Christine screamed as she watched him go, trapped in the firm grip of Edmund Carstairs.

But he was not listening; he could no longer hear her and instead of rescuing her from this madman, he had abandoned her to him.

And he had insulted her! She could scarcely believe it. Not Michael, not kind, considerate Michael, and it was all Edmund's fault. She spun around and slapped his face, as hard as she could, felt the satisfaction as his head was pushed sideways with the blow. But still he did not release her, still his fingers dug into her flesh as he gripped her arm, as she struggled to pull away from him.

"Michael!" She called out once more.

"What do you think you are doing?" Edmund demanded.

"What am I doing? Michael has gone, he believes I betrayed him. Why would you make him think that?"

"Good," he answered with satisfaction. "Let him go. He may even decide to divorce you and there will be nothing then to stand in our way."

"Divorce? I want no divorce. I love Michael."

Edmund was shaking his head and a little grin of disbelief played about his mouth.

"He has turned your head," he said. "I can see that. He has convinced you that you love him, not me, but we both know the truth." He trailed his forefinger between her breasts, down to below her waist and she shuddered, thankful she wore this thick, winter gown. "Deep down in there, you know the truth of it; you know you love me. I have a house now, a small house compared to this it is true, but it will be ours. If the Earl divorces you, we can be married."

She tried to pull away from him again but he would not loosen his grip; he seemed not to notice the tears which were flooding her cheeks. She cursed herself for not putting her boots back on straight away; she wanted to kick out at his shins, but her feet were bare and it was pointless.

"I will never marry you, Edmund," she shouted. "I do not love you! I have never loved you!"

"That is what you think now, but we will soon change all that. I will make you remember what we once had; you have forgotten, that is all."

"We never had a damn thing!"

"You see, I was right. You have forgotten."

She drew a deep breath. She needed to be calm, that was the secret. She would never get through to him while she showed her anger.

"Edmund, it is my fault. I only kept seeing you to annoy my father."

It was a lie, but she hoped it might make him realise she was not worth the trouble. She had kept seeing him because she was a naïve fool who thought he was her friend, the first friend she had ever been allowed to make for herself.

"Is that what His Grace told you?"

"I have a mind of my own," she said. She pulled her arm once more, still trying to get away from him. "Please let go of me. I want to go back to Michael, to my little girl."

He pulled her towards him then, kissed her again while she struggled feebly against his strength. That is what Michael saw, but why the hell did he not see what was really happening? He had always been jealous of Edmund, always believed he forced their marriage on her and nothing she said would change his mind. This is where his jealousy had brought them.

"You will soon forget her," Edmund said. "We can have more children."

"Forget? My child?" She was horrified but he seemed indifferent to anything other than his own goal. "I am her mother; I will never forget her. No other child will ever replace her."

He smiled again. He was obviously intent on ignoring her every objection, pretending she did not mean it, that others had put ideas into her head. How insulting!

"It has all been too much for you," he said. "I understand. Wait until you see the house; you will love it!"

He picked up her velvet cloak from the bed where she had dropped it and draped it around her shoulders, then he gathered up her slippers from the floor, all while still keeping a firm grip on her arm so she could not escape. He ignored her struggles along with her words; both were as feeble and useless as each other.

He put his arm around her waist and held her tightly all the way down the stairs and out to the stables. As they came outside, she looked up to see in the distance her husband riding away, leaving her to her fate, leaving her just when she needed him the most. She would never forgive him, never! This maniac believed she loved him; there was no telling what he would feel himself entitled to.

As they left the house, she looked about, hoping to see somebody, the servants, the stable boys, anybody who might rescue her. The whole place was deserted.

A coach waited, along with a coachman who grinned insolently at her as Edmund pulled her along and pushed her inside.

Christine struggled all the way to Edmund's house, of which he was so proud. She cried out a few times, but the driver seemed not to care. She soon discovered why.

"It is pointless, darling," Edmund told her. "I told him you are my wife, trying to run away with a lover. He agrees you must be brought home. He will not help you."

"Why, Edmund? Why do you want to hurt me?"

"Oh, sweetheart, that is the last thing I want. I have loved you for years, ever since you were a little girl, and I know you were always afraid to show me how you felt because your father is a duke. He is also a bully who cares nothing for his daughter's happiness, only for her titles and possessions."

She shook her head and wondered if there was any point in arguing with him. He had made up his mind this was what she wanted; his own desire was to possess her, to own her, and he would ignore everything she said.

She spent the journey staring out of the carriage window at the passing landscape, hoping to remember where they came, hoping to recognise some part of the scenery so she would know where she was.

It was not a long journey, perhaps an hour or so, and that gave her hope. If she managed to escape it would not be too far to walk back to Melford Hall.

At last the carriage drew to a stop; Christine made no attempt to leave her seat, but Edmund got out and took her arm, pulled her to the ground.

"Please," she cried out to the driver. "This man is trying to abduct me. I am the Countess of Melford; you must get word to my husband."

The infuriating man only smiled.

"His Lordship told me that is what you would say. He told me how you had run away with your lover, Lord Melford's brother. You need to be put in your place, Madam, taught how a woman should behave."

Anger swelled.

"How dare you speak to me like that?" She cried. "When my husband learns of this you will be sorry."

The driver only shook his head and drove away.

Still holding her arm in a firm grip, Edmund began to stride toward the house, dragging her along behind him. That was when she began to worry about the night to come; the man was obviously deranged, believed himself in love with her, even entitled to her. Would he try to force himself on her? She shivered.

She tried once more.

"Edmund, please," she said. "If you ever felt anything for me, you must let me go. I love my husband and my child. I do not want to be here."

His reply was to bend his head and kiss her cheek, then he led her inside the house, where he turned and locked the door, removed the key and put it in his pocket.

There was a fire roaring in the hearth, taking the early evening chill off the air, and he put his arm around her and led her to a chair beside the warmth. She sat on the edge, ready to leap to her feet at the first opportunity.

He brought wine for them both and sat beside her, smiling as his eyes wandered over her.

"At last," he said. "At last I have you here where you belong. What do you think of the house?"

"How did you come by it?"

He laughed, a satisfied laugh as though he had accomplished something wonderful.

"It was fate, my darling. My father died and my brother, Roger inherited. Then he died too so it is all mine."

"Roger was not much older than you. How did he die?"

He had told her before, but she had forgotten and besides, she wanted to keep him talking, hopefully lead him into a conversation which would make him realise what he was doing.

Edmund made no reply for a few seconds, just gazing at her with that little satisfied smile on his face.

"I told you; it was food poisoning."

She asked no more questions, but something told her Roger's demise was no accident. Edmund's next words confirmed her suspicions.

"He was all that stood between us," he said.

"No, he was not all that stood between us."

She caught the rest of her words before they emerged. She was convinced he had killed his brother to get his hands on the family fortune, so he could court Christine.

"Come, you are not drinking," he said. "I have a feast prepared for us, a wedding feast."

"Wedding feast? Edmund, I am already married."

"Not really," he said confidently. "If there is a prior commitment, your marriage can be easily annulled."

She put the goblet down on the hearthstone and got to her feet.

"There was no prior commitment," she said.

He laughed.

"Of course there was. You were betrothed to me, you surely remember. Or has Lord Melford convinced you that it never happened?"

"It never did happen, Edmund. I love Michael, I love my little girl. I want to go home."

"You see, I was right. He has put these ideas into your head." He took her hand and squeezed it, leaned forward and kissed her cheek and she shuddered. "It will not take long to make you remember."

While Edmund led Christine to the table, heavily laden with sumptuous dishes, she wondered if there was another exit from this house besides the door which he had locked. She was angry, both with her abductor and with her husband, and she allowed that anger to fester and grow to give her courage.

"Come, my love," Edmund said. "We will eat, then we will to bed. I cannot tell you how I have longed to hold you in my arms, to make you mine."

"I am not yours, Edmund," she argued, "nor will I ever be. I am married to Michael."

He shrugged.

"That is of no matter. Once he realises you are lost to him, he will likely divorce you and if he does not, we can still be together."

She slammed her knife down on the table, so hard it bounced into the air and landed in the soup.

"What sort of whore do you think I am?" She demanded.

"Whore? It was your husband who used that word, not me. I would never think that of you. That should prove to you that I love you more than he does."

"If I should allow you into my bed I would be just what he accused me of, no better. Do you not see that?"

Edmund smiled, shook his head indulgently as though humouring a child.

"Of course you will not," he said. "You and I, we are meant to be together. No church service can change that. You will see."

That was when she decided there was little point in arguing with him. He would listen to nothing she had to say; he had made up his mind and nothing was going to change it. She had to concentrate on getting away.

"So you would rape me, then?" She demanded, hanging on to that anger despite the pounding in her heart.

"Rape? Of course not. I love you; you love me. It will be a consummation of our love." He stared at her plate, then put down his knife. "You are not eating," he said. "And I spent a fortune on this feast for you."

"I do not feel like eating. I miss my home; I miss my husband and I miss my baby. I want to go home."

It was a final plea. If he ignored such a plea, nothing was going to make him listen and she had to get away. She suspected she was with child; she could not allow this deranged abductor to endanger her child. She was convinced he had murdered his brother in order to have the inheritance for himself; if he would kill his own brother to get what he wanted, there was no telling what he might do to her.

With tremendous effort she stilled her trembling hands; she had to suppress her terror, hold back the tears which were desperate to get out. If he saw how she really felt, he might try to comfort her and she shuddered at the very idea. Or he might grow angry enough to do her some harm. He was already angry because she refused to eat.

He got to his feet and smiled. It was a forced smile; she could see that. He was still angry because she had refused the feast he had prepared.

"Silly," he said. "You are home." He held out his hand to her. "Come, I will show you your bedchamber. Tomorrow I will send for a dressmaker to make you a new trousseau to celebrate our marriage."

She ignored his open hand, remained seated at the table and cursed herself for losing her temper and the knife. She had to do something; the idea of this man doing the things to her that Michael did made her feel sick.

Still he stood with his hand held out, ready to take hers.

"Come," he said. "It is getting late."

She made no move, just stared at him.

"And where will you sleep, Mr Carstairs?"

"A little formal," he replied. "Are you trying to be coy? Come."

"No. I will not come with you."

He reached across the table and grabbed her wrist, his hand clamped tightly around it, as she tried in vain to pull away.

"Let go of me!"

"You will come," he said and he pulled her out of the bench and onto her feet. "You are mine now."

He made his way to the staircase and began to climb, dragging her along behind him. She fought against his strength, tried to hang on to anything that would give her some resistance, but there was nothing. There was no banister rail, nothing but the original stone from which the house was built, and it was shiny with nothing to grip and hold on to.

Inside the bedchamber, candles were already lit, a fire roared brightly and flowers were entwined around the bedposts. She turned to face him; would knowing her condition stop him? Or would it inflame him even more? And did she really want him to know about her baby? What might he do to it if she could not escape before the birth?

"Edmund, you killed your brother, you killed Roger. Am I right?"

He smiled, a satisfied smile as though expecting congratulations.

"I did it for you," he said. "I did it for us."

"There is no 'us'!"

His face darkened in anger.

"He stood between us; I had no choice."

Christine stood silently watching him, her heart hammering wildly and wondering what on earth she could say or do to make this man understand she did not want him. She was such a fool! She thought she knew Edmund, thought he at least cared about her as a friend. Now she knew he had murdered his brother she was terrified of what he would do if she did manage to convince him. And why did neither he nor Michael listen to her?

Edmund's arm went around her and he began to walk with her toward the bed.

"I am not sharing that bed with you, Mr Carstairs," she said firmly.

His fingers clenched on her shoulder, dug painfully into the flesh; his face wore a scowl of anger.

"Will you stop calling me that?"

"It seems more appropriate."

He loosened his grip and smiled, his eyes widened as though he had an idea that would solve all their problems.

"Forgive me," he said. "I should have realised. You are a virtuous woman; you do not feel you are free to give yourself to another man while Lord Melford lives."

She stiffened, her heart leapt, threatening to choke her and her eyes widened with shock.

"What do you mean?"

"I have killed for you, but I have not removed the real obstacle to our happiness. How remiss of me. All I can say in my defence is that I was anxious to have you to myself."

"No!" She was shaking her head, frantic to find something to say to deter him from this path. "Please do not hurt Michael."

"But it is what we want."

"No. I do not want my daughter to grow up an orphan; you must understand, please. I will do whatever you want, but please do not hurt Michael."

He pulled her into his arms and pressed her head against his chest while she tried to hide her disgust.

"Anything I want?" He murmured.

He began to unfasten her gown. The urge to pull away, the need to shudder were almost irresistible, but she knew she had to pretend to want this. There was no alternative now, as her words had fallen on deaf ears.

She pushed gently at his chest, looked up him.

"Not now," she said through mounting fear. "Tomorrow."

"Why? Why should we wait until tomorrow? I have everything prepared."

She took a deep breath to give her courage.

"Have you no idea of how a woman's body works?"

His eyes moved over her suspiciously, then at last he smiled. He pulled her closer and kissed her lips, a long kiss filled with desire which made her catch back a sob. Even his most passionate kiss could not compare to Michael's. When he released her, she fought the urge to wipe her mouth.

He looked down at her face, wiped the tears from her cheeks with his fingers.

"What is this?" He said. "Tears? You love me that much?"

She stood rigidly, desperately hoping he would go. She needed to think, needed to find a way to escape this place, to get home to Melford Hall, to get back to London somehow. But it was spring; very soon Michael and his brothers would return to Essex for the summer, then she would be safe at least, if not happy.

Why the hell did Michael not realise Edmund was forcing his kisses on her? Why did he not stop when she called him back? She was uncertain which hurt more, Michael's abandonment or Edmund's insistence that she was in love with him.

At last Edmund released her, kissed her cheek affectionately and left the chamber. The first thing she did was look to see if he had left a key in the lock, but there was nothing. She moved to the door, but as she got close she heard the key turn. She was trapped.

She sank down onto the bed and cried herself to sleep.

***

It was not quite dawn when she awoke. The fire had died, she felt the chill in the air and a glance from the window told her the sun was not quite winning its battle for daylight. She picked up her cloak and wrapped herself in it, moved to the window and looked out at the wakening farmland outside.

From here she could see the milk maids making their way into the sheds to relieve the cows of their milk. It would be very cold out there so early and certainly not somewhere Christine wanted to be had she a choice, but she did not.

She stood watching for a few more minutes. The only people about were farmworkers and if she could get the window to open, she could be long gone before Edmund woke up. Was he likely to lay abed and anticipate what he thought would be his that night? At least Michael was still in London and she thought it unlikely that Edmund would go that far to attack him, but he would be here soon enough and she had to escape before that happened.

She cursed herself for being such a poor judge of character, she wondered how any man could think so highly of himself as to ignore her wishes, believe them not to be real because they conflicted with his.

Michael had also ignored her pleas, but he had a different motive. He believed she loved Edmund; how could he think that? How could he believe she would betray her marriage vows? Had she not shown him how much he meant to her?

She recalled the nights they had spent together, recalled how she had allowed her love to show in every way possible. The need to kiss his muscular chest had been irresistible and she had never fought against that need. Why should she? They were lawfully married in the sight of God and she loved him, for heaven's sake! What more could she have done to show him that?

The dart of anger pierced her again but she had no time to deal with it now. She had to get away; she stroked the very slight bulge of her stomach. Very soon she would be too bulky to climb out of the window; it was barely wide enough for her now. She needed to escape before tonight, before Edmund came, wanting her to fulfil her promise.

She pulled a red woollen blanket from the bed and swept it over her head and shoulders. She did not want to shiver in just the velvet cloak and besides, she thought she would be less conspicuous in the blanket. It would make her look like a peasant, and Edmund would not be searching for a peasant.

The window opened easily, much to her relief. Of course, her gaoler would not expect a lady such as herself to even think of climbing out of a window. If he read his mythology he would find it had been done many times in fables.

It was a long way up and she was terrified of falling and harming her unborn child, if child there should be. But not as terrified as she was of the man who had brought her here, the man she had believed to be her friend. And she said a silent prayer of thanks that she had not been born with a fear of heights.

There was a tree only two or three feet from the window. It was a solid oak tree, certainly strong enough to take her weight. She looked across at the landscape once more, searching for the stables, hoping there might be a horse she could steal or even a donkey. But there would be stable boys sleeping in there, stable boys loyal to Edmund.

She pulled her skirts up and tied them into a knot about her waist, then took one step out of the window and rested her foot on the ledge. Her heart quivered, but she would not be deterred. Better to fall, to risk breaking her neck than submit to Edmund's demands.

She almost slipped reaching out to grab the branch of the tree, but managed to save herself. Now she stopped and watched carefully to be sure she was not being observed. Everybody was too busy with their own duties to even notice that someone was climbing out of an upstairs window and they were all too far away to see her in the half light.

Having grazed her legs while sliding down the bark of the tree trunk, she was relieved to have two feet on the ground, despite that ground being covered in dew and soaking her feet through the thin slippers. She untied her skirts and felt their warmth around her legs. Snuggled into the velvet cloak and the blanket, she began to run toward the barns and out of sight of the house.

She waited a little while longer, just to be sure Edmund was not following, but obviously it was yet too early for him to be about. She ran as quickly as she could away from the farm and into the forest, where she found cover among the trees.

***

Christine was exhausted by the time she reached Melford Hall. Her back ached, her legs ached and her anger with Michael was equal to her anger with Edmund. They had both put her through this, both thinking they knew her better than she knew herself, and if her child was harmed because of it she would never forgive Michael.

Edmund needed to be brought to trial for the murder of his brother, if not for her abduction, but Michael had seriously let her down. His jealousy and distrust had brought her to this and she was not sure if she could ever forgive him. She would never forget the hurt when he left; she could not believe he had turned away from her, had abandoned her when she had been thinking he had come to save her. Yet she clung to that hurt now as she made her way through the trees, clung to it to fuel her anger and give her the courage to go on.

She emerged from the forest behind the stables and looked longingly towards the House with its soft beds, its hearths which she would have lit as soon as possible, the kitchens and the good meat. She hoped the servants were still there. There were just a few, but enough to make Christine comfortable.

When she was fully recovered she would send word to Michael in London that she was here and needed to talk to him. She was sure he would come, regardless of his parting insult. He would have had time to calm himself and listen to what she had to say.

But as her eyes moved over the house, her heart almost stopped in her chest. There was Edmund, sitting on the steps beside the front door, his mare tied loosely to a tree as she munched the grass.

Christine almost cried out. He had guessed where she would be and had got here before her; now she had nowhere to go. The Manor House was still being renovated so there were workmen there. They did not know her and Edmund had managed to convince the coachman that she was his wife; he would likely have no problem convincing the builders of the same.

She fled behind the stable block before she was seen, leaned against the stone wall and slid down to sit, exhausted, on the hard, cold ground, as she tried to decide where she should go, what she should do. One of the villagers might take her in, but they likely believed she had run away with a lover. It had happened only yesterday, but gossip of this calibre spread like wildfire. It was also possible that Edmund could buy information from any one of them if they were desperate enough.

She fought back tears of despair, swallowed the massive ache in her throat and tried to hang on to her anger. She would sleep in one of the barns if necessary, but with Edmund guarding the doors, who knew that he would start a search for her?

It was like a sign from Heaven when she suddenly remembered the derelict fishing village down on the cliff. It was shelter if nothing else and the stable block stood between the house and the beach. She would not need to show herself to get there and she began to make her way towards it, looking back every few minutes to be sure she was not followed.

She had come here once with Michael, during the first week of their marriage when he was showing her his estate. He had told her then how dangerous the place was and made her promise never to go there alone, but now she had no choice but to break that promise.

At last she arrived at the cottage on the cliff top. At least it was still intact and would give her somewhere to rest until Edmund went away.

The cottage was built from stones gathered from various places around the coast. The thatch on the roof was in good repair at least. It would be dry inside, if nothing else, and her one consolation was that this disaster had not occurred during the winter months. With the summer fast approaching, she should be able to stay here until the family returned from London.

It was very sparse, but there were two rooms and in the corner of one was a roughly made wooden bed with a straw mattress. She breathed a sigh of relief as she took off her wet slippers and lie down on the low bed, not something she was accustomed to but she was so weary anything would have done. She still had some money in her purse which she had brought with her to give to the mother of the newborn child to whom Christine should have been godmother.

She could perhaps get to the village on market day unrecognised.

She did not feel secure enough to sleep, but she was too exhausted to stay awake and despite her efforts, she slept until morning.

***

The preparations for Grace's wedding were still going ahead, despite the condition she had imposed. James was furious about his brother's reaction to that condition; he thought he should ignore the girl, carry on as though she had said nothing, but Michael would not have it. James was sure it was because he really wanted to find the whore himself, wanted an excuse to bring her home. If only he had done so when he first found her with her lover, not waited until she was damaged goods, they would not be going to all this trouble now.

He remembered that day, when Michael returned to his London house without his wife, how angry James had been.

"Where is Christine?" He asked.

Michael made no reply while he went to pour ale and take it to a chair. James watched him for a few seconds, knowing something horrendous had occurred but not wanting to push him. His brother was the most placid man James had ever known, but he did have a temper, even if it was slow to waken.

"I found them together in her bedchamber," Michael said at last, his mouth forming a bitter line. "She was locked in the arms of Edmund Carstairs."

"What!"

"They were kissing, James. He had his arms around her. It seems you were right; she did go there to meet him."

Michael's voice faded as it choked on unshed tears, a sight James hoped never to see again. But that sight made him so angry, he wanted to kill Christine himself. Had she been there, he did not think he would have been able to help himself.

"And you left her there?" He demanded.

Michael's eyes met his and he swallowed more ale.

"Yes, I left her there," he answered at last. "It is obvious what she wants. She has always loved him and I tore her away from him. I thought I could just come along and force her into a marriage she did not want, buy her favours like I bought this house, like I bought my horse. It is my own fault if I am paying now for my arrogance in thinking her just another possession."

"Michael you are a fool! She is your wife; she is a possession whether you want to admit it or not."

"No, James. I could never think of her as that, not now. I love her. I want nothing but her happiness and if that happiness lies with him, so be it."

James snatched the tankard out of his brother's hand and slammed it down, took his wrist and pulled him out of his chair.

"You need to get her back, before it is too late, if it is not already too late. You need to bring her back here, lock her up till she learns her proper place, with a good beating to help her understand."

That was when Michael's slumbering temper flamed and he punched his brother square on the jaw. As he fell to the polished, wooden floor, James slid across it and banged his head on the wall behind him, but he felt a little smile forming on his lips.

He had finally managed to rouse some proper feeling in Michael at least, even if he had gone too far.

That had been earlier in the year, after the Easter festival. Now it was almost the end of the summer, some six months later, and they had heard nothing since. James would have been content for Christine never to be mentioned again; he wanted Michael to divorce her, but that would mean a charge of adultery and he would never do that.

Now he had made up his mind he would have to find her, just to appease the whim of another young woman, their young sister.

"I shall have to go to Baron Carstairs' manor house," Michael told his brother. "If they are not there, he might be persuaded to tell me where they are. I have no idea where else to start looking."

"I am surprised you have not been there already," James replied. "If she were my wife…"

"Yes, James, we know what you would have done had she been your wife."

For all James' threats and blustering, Michael was quite sure he had never raised a hand to Helen. He could tell by her demeanour she was not afraid of her husband; in fact she seemed quite devoted to him, although Michael could never understand why. If he thought for one moment his brother had ever carried out his threats, he would have to interfere. He could not have a man like that living in his house, even if he was his brother.

John had been sitting with them, listening to their plans to find Christine and bring her home. Neither of them seemed to notice he was there, listening, but that was nothing unusual. The more they said, the more his heart sank.

Now he got to his feet and took his wine to the window to stare out toward the sea on the horizon. He wanted to escape; he could not allow Michael to go searching for his wife, to suffer the humiliation of asking Carstairs for her whereabouts, not when John knew where she was. But he had promised her he would keep her whereabouts a secret and he had kept his word for Michael's sake, because he did not want his brother to know about the child.

He had questioned Christine when he returned to her that first day, but she had refused to tell him anything.

"It is not your business, John," she told him. "You have never been in love. You know nothing of the pain you can feel when the one you love turns his back on you, just when you need him the most. I am grateful for your help, of course I am, but that help does not give you leave to know my private life."

"Michael would want to know. My sister, too, will want to know."

"Ah, Grace," she murmured softly. "Yes, I do so miss Grace. And Lisa; please tell me my little girl is thriving."

"She is; I would have told you else. You must miss her."

"Of course I miss her! I am her mother."

"Then how could you run away with your lover and leave her?"

Those tears welled up again, making him wish he had never asked.

"I had no choice, John. I would never have left my baby if I had a choice."

"Then why will you not let me tell Michael where you are?"

She glanced down at herself and cradled her womb protectively with both hands.

"Because I do not want to have to miss this one as well," she said.

She was likely right; Michael might well take Christine back as his wife, try to forgive her and put her sins behind them, but he could not be expected to take her bastard child as well. He would send it back to its father, or take it away, foster it out, find it a good home, yes, but allow her to keep the baby? That would be too much to ask, even of a man of Michael's generous nature.

John had always been fond of Christine, ever since Michael married her; she was a kind woman and gracious. He was shocked when he learned what had happened and while he wanted to comfort her now, memories of the hurt she had caused his brother stood in his way.

As he rode back to the house after settling Christine into the Manor House, he realised this secret was going to be almost impossible to keep. He had not asked too much about the child; why should he? He knew it was not of his brother's making and it was that alone which enforced his promise to keep Christine's whereabouts a secret. Michael would be destroyed to know his wife might give her lover the son she had failed to give him.

Now as he stood with his back to his two elder brothers and listened to the conversation going on behind him, he knew he no longer had a choice. He would have to tell Michael where she was, or fetch her himself. He decided on the latter.

It had been but a few months ago when he found Christine, yet it seemed like years since this heavy weight had settled itself on his shoulders; he could not deny he was anxious to be rid of it. He remembered the half hearted plans he had made to leave Melford, to seek adventure abroad or in the north and his heart skipped. He allowed a small smile to creep over his lips at the thought of finally being free, having never before realised he was anything else.

He tossed back the goblet and drained it, wishing he had never gone to the cliff edge that day, wishing he had taken himself up north as he had intended and never found Christine and her bastard child.

He knew the two men were taking no notice of him, were not even concerned about his opinion. He was the youngest son, elder only to his sister. They had never been particularly concerned with John's opinions, so talking in front of him was not something they would avoid. And it was certain they would never suspect that he knew the answer to their dilemma.

Christine's hiding place could stay secret no longer.

CHAPTER FIVE

Christine sat in the empty Manor House and imagined the welcome she might get if she were to return to Melford Hall. Since she had seen Michael and his family return from London in the spring, she had thought often how it would be.

She thought it likely she would have to return, even if John did manage to gather enough funds to pay for a midwife. She really would rather not have her baby here, alone with nobody who loved her, nobody who cared whether she survived the birth or not. When Lisa was born she had Helen for company, Michael waited in the next chamber to see if his child was safe and well. He had been equally anxious to learn that his wife was safe and well.

When she first suspected the seeding of this child, before Edmund came and spoilt everything, she had so looked forward to seeing the joy on Michael's face, she had prayed it would be a son. Now everything had changed, because everyone would assume this child was not her husband's, even him. She cared little for the opinions of the others, but not Michael. She could not bear for Michael to think that. And what would happen to the child if he never learned to accept it?

That was her reason for wanting to keep her whereabouts a secret, that whilst she was lying helpless from the birth, her child might be taken away and fostered out, because everyone thought they knew it was not Michael's.

The ancient fishing village had not survived the winter storms, so why the cottage had she could not tell. It must have been damaged over the years and she worried if it would cope with any more damage. She wondered if she and her baby would be swept over the cliff along with it. But while Edmund lurked about, waiting to pounce on her and drag her back to his fantasy world where she belonged to him, there was nowhere else for her to hide. Its best feature was its distance from the house, the stables and all the other buildings where people were likely to see her.

She was relieved when John found her, when he brought her here to the Manor House. She would have tried to break into this house when she first escaped from Edmund, but she knew the workmen had not finished and she had no idea about the priest's holes.

Even with John's help, she could not have this baby here, alone. Was her pride worth such a risk? She had no claim on him; she could hardly expect him to look after her for the next few years and James would want the house back at some point.

What would she do when the child got too heavy to carry in a sling about her shoulders? How would she keep a toddler from going outside and showing himself? That would be cruel, to deny a growing child the sunlight.

All these problems whirled about her mind while she fought to find solutions to them, yet not a mile away stood a luxurious country mansion with many rooms, polished floorboards and thick rugs from Persia. There would be servants to bring water to bathe the baby, seamstresses to make new clothes for her and her child, and it was a home to which they were both entitled. And in that house was her little girl, her baby daughter from whom Edmund had torn her away and Michael had let him.

That last thought brought a swell of anger which threatened to consume her and she felt her hands clenching into fists against her will. She wanted to hit him, to slap his face for allowing this to happen to her, when he should have known better.

Bitter tears welled up as she pulled her woollen cloak closer around her shoulders and thought about her future. Had John never found her, she would have been forced to appeal to Michael long before this. John could have no idea that keeping her secret helped her to stay hidden, but it could not go on for much longer.

She had to swallow her pride and think first of her child, of what was best for her new son or daughter, and she would have to persuade Michael to give that child a place in his house. Yet she should not have to do that, he should not need to be persuaded, and the knowledge that he did made her furious again.

She loved Michael, had loved him since the day of their marriage but he had hurt her badly by turning away when she needed him, no matter what his reasons.

He was the sweetest man, the kindest man, but even he might find it hard to believe this child was his. People thought her so fortunate to have married a man like Michael, yet had he not been such a man, she might never have been put in this position in the first place.

She blamed him for that; she could not help it. She was so angry with him for leaving her, for not listening to her explanation, for not fighting for her, she was not sure she could ever forgive him.

Now she sat and thought about her life before he left her, thought about how she had accepted him as her husband without a protest. She married him because she was told to marry him; she had no choice. Oh, she could have refused, but her father was not a man to accept defiance, not a man on whom she could make demands. Michael applied to him for his daughter's hand in marriage and he had agreed without a word to her.

The day the Duke sent for her to come to his private study would always remain clear in her memory. He told her of his decision, how he had accepted the Earl of Melford for his daughter. The interview, if interview it was, lasted but a few minutes. His Grace told her nothing else, nothing about the man, about his age, his looks, nothing.

"I have accepted an offer for your hand in marriage," he said. "Your future husband is the Earl of Melford; he has but recently come into the title, having lost both his father and elder brother in an accident. He tells me he noticed you at Her Majesty's coronation, but had little to offer at the time. You should be flattered."

Her thoughts raced as she tried to drag up an image of the event and the men who were present, hoping for a memory of anyone who had perhaps paid her extra attention, but there was nothing. She was too entranced with the elaborate clothing worn by the new Queen and the excitement of being there, in Westminster Hall, to notice much else and now she was being told she was to marry a man she had never laid eyes on. He could be an old man for all she knew, for all her father would care.

"What age is this man?" She asked.

The Duke raised an eyebrow, frowned as though surprised that she should ask such a question, and he probably was. She did not think she had ever questioned him before, on any subject. In fact, she could barely remember talking to him at all. It was unlikely he had ever considered what it meant to be a woman, to be bedded by a man she had never met and one who was perhaps fat and wrinkled. He was a man and a man could bed any woman without a thought.

He shrugged.

"I suppose he is in his early twenties."

She breathed a sigh of relief then left the room. There followed weeks of dressmakers, hairdressers and sample fabrics, jewellers with precious gems for her trousseau, all of whom served to distract her from the apprehension of what her future might hold with this stranger. She was not even to be given a portrait of him.

"Can I not see him, Father?" She had asked. "Just to see what he looks like."

"Whatever for? You are betrothed; nothing will alter that, so what difference does it make what he looks like?"

He had strolled away from her, shaking his head as though she were a child asking for some unattainable toy. Had her mother lived, she would have understood Christine's anxiety. Had she not made her father promise not to marry their daughter too early? But she had not lived, she had died of a fever when Christine was but eight years old.

Christine was taught from birth that she was a very important lady and she would be told who her friends were to be, what she was to wear, how to conduct herself and who she would marry. She never questioned it, but as reality closed in she found herself very nervous. She knew it was a good match and she knew her father would send her off to a convent if she did not agree. There were Lutheran convents now, where once there had been only Catholic ones, but it made no difference to Christine. She wanted a husband, a home and children; she had no wish to spend her life kneeling on cold stone and praying for what? She wondered for the first time just what those nuns found to pray about. It was not for a lover, a husband or children, it was not for vast wealth and lands. She could see no point to it and she would rather be married to the stranger who had asked.

At least this earl had been attracted to her, not her lands or her dowry. That gave her hope of a sort.

The betrothal was informal, settled between her father and Michael and they did not meet before the wedding. She was nervous, of course she was, but it was only what other maidens had experienced in the past. In all honesty she would be happy to be away from the Duke's bullying manner; he ordered her every move, even told her how to wear her hair and what gowns to wear. She hoped her husband would not be of the same temperament, but even if he was, she would at least be mistress in her own household.

Edmund Carstairs proved to be more of a threat than she had anticipated. He had been paying court to her over the previous months in an informal way. She was so naïve, she thought he was just being friendly; she had no idea he was thinking in terms of a relationship, a marriage even. If she had, she would have told him it would never be allowed. He had made no application to her father and had he done so, he would have been refused permission to pursue her. He was the youngest son of a baron and had nothing, he was certainly not good enough for the daughter of a Duke.

He was a nice enough young man. He had turned up at various balls with his older brother and Christine had given little thought to how he got there, whether he had been invited. He often appeared in the grounds when she was walking there and asked to walk with her. She saw no reason to refuse him; she had not seen what was happening. She was pleased to have a friend she had chosen for herself for the first time in her life.

The Duke saw them walking together once and sent a servant to call her back to the house.

"Did you invite that young man here?" He demanded.

"No, Father. He often comes to see me. I thought you knew."

The Duke scowled.

"No, I most certainly did not know. If he comes again, you are to tell him he is not welcome."

"Why? He is but a friend."

"Friend is he? I choose your friends, not you. It is obvious to me that young Edmund Carstairs has ideas above his station."

"What does that mean?"

"Never mind what it means. You are to discourage him, do you understand me?"

She had nodded her agreement, as there was little point in arguing with him, but she did not believe he was right. She was not going to be rude to Edmund and telling him he was unwelcome would have been just that.

But when she told him she was promised to Michael, Earl of Melford, his face had darkened in anger as he bit down on his lip.

"You cannot marry him!" He shouted.

Christine leapt back, startled.

"What are you talking about?" She said, trying hard to hold on to her composure. "It is settled; my father has promised me to him."

"And you have no say in the matter?"

"Of course not." She watched him silently, watched his expression harden even further and looked around to see if there were anyone to help should she need it. "Edmund, you did not think…?"

"Think what? That you might want to marry me? I know you love me."

She shook her head.

"If I loved you, I would be distressed, I would be resisting this marriage. I am doing neither. No, I do not love you. I thought we were friends, nothing more."

He turned and clutched at her arms, pulled her roughly toward him.

"Come away with me," he said. "We can elope, run away together. Perhaps we can find a ship, go to the Americas, anywhere so long as we are together."

She pushed him away.

"I do not want to go to the Americas," she said. "I do not want to marry you."

For the first time since she had met Edmund, she was afraid of him. His strength was too much for her to resist, that was apparent as he pulled her along while she struggled to hold back.

"You would rather wed a man you have never met, one you know nothing about?" He tightened his grip on her arm and began to walk in long strides toward the village, out of sight of the house, dragging her along with him. "You will come with me now. We will run away together, we will be married. By the end of the week you will be my wife."

She almost managed to pull herself away, but his grip tightened even more.

"Edmund! You are hurting me! Let go of me, please!"

"No. You have no idea what you want. I know you love me, as I love you."

She tried to dig her heels into the soft turf, tried to resist his strength, but she had nothing to hold onto and she only stumbled and would have fallen had he not kept his firm grip on her.

"Edmund! Let go of me, now, please!"

That was when two of the manservants saw them. They had been walking in the gardens, just talking and resting from their duties as the Duke allowed, when they noticed Lady Christine being pulled against her will. They heard her cry out, heard her plea for release and ran toward her.

"My Lady," one said. "Do you need assistance?"

"Yes, Martin, please," she sobbed, then she pulled away again. This time Edmund released her, likely seeing himself outnumbered.

He eyed the two servants warily for a few moments, then turned and strode toward the stables where he had left his horse.

"Have no fear, Christine," he called back over his shoulder. "I will return for you."

The two servants escorted her back to the house. She was shaking and tears were gathering in her eyes, and she could do nothing to hold on to her dignity. At last they reached the main doors and she stopped and turned to them.

"Thank you," she said. "Please do something else for me. Do not tell His Grace about this."

"But, My Lady, he should be told. Something should be done about that young man."

"No, please. He will blame me." She could see their expressions were doubtful, but she was afraid of her father finding out. He had explicitly told her to have nothing to do with Edmund and he had been right. "Please. He will say I must have encouraged him, and perhaps I did; I do not know. He might accuse me of all sorts of things."

"Very well, My Lady. If that is what you want, we promise. But you need to be careful to make certain you always have company wherever you go, at least until your marriage."

She nodded, forced a smile and retreated to her bedchamber. They were right; she would have to stay inside the house, make quite sure Edmund never had an opportunity to be alone with her, to try to abduct her again.

Her heart was hammering as she lie on her bed and tried to calm herself, tried to recover from the shock of what had happened. Edmund had thought she loved him? How could that be? She had never given him the slightest indication that she felt anything for him other than friendship. And while she sympathised, she could not help being angry at the way he had tried to drag her away against her will. She had never been so frightened in her life.

What would have happened had the servants not come along to help? Would he have taken her away somewhere, forced himself on her? She was shaking and tears began to seep from her eyes; worst of all, she had no one to talk to, no one who would be sympathetic without blame.

Her brother was of no use; he would agree with the Duke, that she should never have been talking to Edmund in the first place. He always agreed with the Duke, about everything. She wished she had a mother, or a sister, or even a female friend. But no one had ever been good enough to consort with the Duke's daughter and she was not allowed to be familiar with the servants. That was why she had encouraged Edmund, she supposed, because for the first time in her life, she had a friend.

***

The first glimpse she had of Michael was in the candlelit semi-darkness of the church as he waited for her to approach the altar, waited for her to stand beside him and pledge herself to him for life. He turned and smiled as her steps halted next to him and she took note of the warmth in that smile, of the kindness in his blue eyes. The flickering candles made little lights in his hair, making it look gold, although it was blonde, like hers, and he was so tall her head reached only as far as his chest.

The service was in English, from Thomas Cranmer's Book of Common Prayer, and Christine found that comforting. At least she knew what she was promising, even if she had no real idea of why.

After the service, Michael took her hand to lead her out of the church, a gesture she found endearing and although they had spoken not a word to each other, she felt she knew him well already.

He was a handsome man. She would thank her father for that if she thought for one moment he had even noticed, but Michael was very handsome. He had golden hair, a sort of dark blonde, and he was clean shaven, which was not the normal fashion for men. Later, when she asked him about it, he said he found hair on his face to be uncomfortable and he thought he looked better without.

"Of course, if you do not agree," he said with a warm smile, "I will happily grow it again."

It was a glorious day. There was feasting and dancing and lots of food and mead; it was Christine's first taste of honey mead and she thought she could easily learn to like it. Queen Elizabeth sent her blessings and a gift of a huge dish of solid gold. Apparently someone had told Her Majesty that the couple had met at her coronation, so she thought she should notice them.

She also claimed the right to be godmother to their first born son, a prospect Christine found a little daunting and as a token of their gratitude, their first child was named for the Queen, although they always used the derivative of 'Lisa'. Christine was relieved Elizabeth had not invited herself to the wedding; it would have changed the entire atmosphere, taken all the attention from the newly married couple.

Late in the evening, while the minstrels still played and the guests still danced, Michael had taken her hand and led her out of the great hall.

She had heard about this, heard how all the guests followed the newly married couple to their bedchamber and even undressed them. She had heard that they sometimes stayed to watch and she was thrilled when Michael noticed her shiver and put his arm around her.

She glanced back as they approached the staircase, afraid to see a crowd of people clambering up the stairs behind them, but the servants were blocking the doorway, holding back the guests who were trying their best to get to the stairs.

She looked up at Michael and smiled.

"Thank you," she said.

"You are very welcome."

She had fallen in love with him that night. He had been so tender, so considerate; he had undressed her and caressed her and made her want him, had taken her maidenhead in the gentlest way he could and she could not wait to begin their life together.

As she lie in his arms after, she grabbed hold of the memories of what had just happened before they faded or were buried beneath newer memories. She had never felt anything like this before and she knew instinctively that no matter how good it was hereafter, there would never be anything like the first time.

She lie with her head resting on his naked chest, his arms around her, and she could feel the muscles in that arm cushioning her head. She raised her eyes to Michael's face and saw that he was looking down at her and smiling.

It had all gone wrong after her daughter was born and Edmund Carstairs reappeared.

***

Christine managed to hide away in one of the larger of the priest's holes whenever the caretakers from the village arrived. She had a good idea of what day and what time they would appear, so it was not difficult.

The largest of the spaces was a little room where she could stand upright and it was furnished with a chair and a narrow bed, ready for a priest who might need a long stay.

But one day she had to hide in a hurry when she heard the familiar voice of Helen, along with two men from the main house. She squashed herself into the nearest secret space, which was beneath the staircase and she had to fold herself up to stay hidden.

Helen was giving the men instructions on preparing the house for the guests who were expected for Grace's wedding, giving orders to the maids about preparing the bedchambers.

Christine knew her hiding place was safe no longer and that caused her to think more about the sort of welcome she would get at Melford Hall, when she finally appealed to Michael. And she had to appeal to Michael; there was no other way. She was heavy with child, would need confinement and midwives and he certainly owed her those things, even if he did not realise it.

It was so quiet here in the Manor House that when the wind was still, Christine could hear things a long way off. She heard the horse while John was still some half a mile away; she had been putting her meagre belongings into a bundle, ready to take with her when she went back to Melford Hall. She was preparing to walk there, even though she would be seen by everyone who was working outside or perhaps looking out of the windows. What would Michael say, if he glanced out and saw her approaching? Would he be happy to see her or would he refuse such a meeting? What would James say if he were the one to see her? She could imagine he would take it upon himself to greet her with threats and refuse her entry.

She knew nothing of the quarrels between the two brothers about her, nothing about the physical blows they had come to. Whatever happened, she had to face it. It could not be long now, and she wanted to be ready. She stopped what she was doing and went to the door to watch John's approach.

When he dismounted he seemed agitated and unusually had brought nothing with him, no supplies of food or ale, nothing. He strode toward the house as though he was trying his best not to break into a run. Something had made him come here in a hurry and she was not sure she wanted to know what it was.

She turned away and went inside.

"Christine, it is over," he told her as he followed her into the house. "Michael is planning to find you. He is going to Carstairs Manor this very afternoon."

"Why? Why does he want to find me after all this time?"

"Grace is to be married."

"I know that. Do you think I have not watched her at every opportunity? Besides, Helen was here last week giving orders about preparing the place for guests. I had to stay in a priest's hole for hours and it was very cramped."

John took a deep breath.

"My sister has declared she will not marry her Viscount unless you are there to see it."

For the first time since he had found her, she laughed, and it was not a bitter laugh, but a laugh of joy.

"Good for her. A girl after my own heart."

"I will have to tell Michael where you are," he said. "I cannot in all conscience allow him to go to Edmund Carstairs in search of his own wife; it would be too humiliating. Nor can I allow him to worry when he learns you are not there, not when I know the answer. I shall tell him on my return."

As he turned away, she touched his arm to stop him.

"No," she said. "I will come with you."

His eyes swept her swollen stomach, his mouth turned down.

"What about the baby?" He asked.

"What about it?"

John did not answer for a few seconds, as though afraid he might say the wrong thing.

"I rather wanted time to break it to him before he saw you," John said sheepishly. "I have kept it to myself because it is what you wanted and because I could not bear for him to know. You have hurt him enough, Christine; he does not deserve to meet with his wife after such a breach only to see she is carrying another man's child."

Those treacherous tears rose up again, but this time she fought them with her wrath. This was an example of how she would be treated on her return, what she was to look forward to, from James, from Helen, even from the servants. It was intolerable!

And Michael? Would he also treat her with such disdain? Christine could stand everyone else's disrespect, but not his. Not Michael's.

"Why are you so certain it is another man's child?" She demanded angrily.

John studied her face, his eyes sweeping her figure again as he frowned.

"Are you saying it is not?"

She sighed and shook her head.

"Is there a point to this conversation? If you do not believe me, how will I ever convince your brother? If you tell him before he sees me, he will know your opinion, he will never believe this child is his."

"I do not understand. I do not understand how you could have done this to him, the kindest man who ever lived. Now you tell me you have been living with Carstairs whilst carrying Michael's child?"

"I did not tell you I was living with Edmund," she said. "That was your own idea."

"It was what Michael told us. He said he found the two of you kissing in your bedchamber. When he returned to the house, you had gone with Carstairs. Someone told him they had seen you riding away in his carriage." He paused and caught his breath to calm himself; each word he spoke made him angrier. "Do you have another explanation?"

"Yes, John, I do. But that explanation is Michael's, not yours."

She said no more, even though he waited. After a moment, he scowled as he picked up the bundle of clothes she had put together. This was just what he had been avoiding all these months, that his brother should learn of his wife's condition, but there seemed nothing he could do to avoid it.

Outside he lifted her onto his horse and swung himself up into the saddle behind her. He held her tight to prevent her from falling, his arms around her swelling figure, felt the little flutters of the unborn child and fury swept away all thoughts of kindness toward her. Had he not known that Michael would never forgive him, he thought he would strangle her there and then. Treacherous whore she may be, but she was still his brother's wife.

***

"Do you want me to come with you?" James asked.

The two men still sat together; neither of them had noticed John's departure from the house, they had been too engrossed in the immediate problem of whether to look for Christine or disappoint their little sister.

"No," Michael replied. "It would be better if I went alone. You will only lose your temper and make the situation worse."

James shook his head in disgust.

"It might not be a bad thing if you were to lose your temper occasionally," James replied. "If you had, your wife might have found more respect for you than to run off with another man."

"It was losing my temper which made me leave her to him. How can that be a good thing? Had I not done so, I might have kept her with me."

"No." James shook his head. "You would not have kept her with you. You let her go to him because it was what she wanted and you are a fool for her; you gave her everything she wanted."

"Perhaps I am a fool, but I would give anything to have her back."

James sighed impatiently.

"I do not understand how you can face the humiliation of asking your wife's lover for her whereabouts. She is not worth it! It makes me angry just thinking about it."

"It is not a task I relish, James, believe me. But I do want her back, you are right. I will forgive her, I will take her back in my house. Whether I will take her back in my bed is another matter, one I cannot even think about."

CHAPTER SIX

Riding over the rough ground in front of John's saddle was uncomfortable and Christine thanked God the journey was a short one. At least she would not be recognised, wrapped up in a red wool blanket and travelling like this. She felt his heart beating against her back where he held tight to her, to keep her from falling, and she wondered if perhaps she should have explained to him. But he had already decided her guilt, just as Michael had and it was pointless. It was between her and her husband, not for anyone else.

When they arrived at the house, John dismounted and reached up to lift her down from the horse. She spied a stable boy running up to take the reins and pulled her hood closer about her face as she turned her back on him. She did not want the whole estate to know she was here before Michael knew it and servants were notorious gossips.

She stood and looked longingly at the massive house, the house Michael had ordered built specially for them to begin their marriage, the house she had always loved, and her lips quivered. What would happen when he saw her? Could she convince him of the truth? Or would she be banished from his house, sent to live in some small manor somewhere where he would never need to look at her. The memory of his anger the last time she had seen him rose up and she could think of nothing but the harsh words he had spoken. She had never known Michael to lose his temper before, certainly not with her, and it was so unfair!

Her eyes filled with tears again and she pushed the memory away as she turned to John, gripping his arm. Despite her anger and resentment, she could not bear for Michael to be hurt, and the shock of seeing her like this would hurt him.

"You are right," she told John. "Tell him before I see him. But tell him nothing else, please."

"Very well."

"Do you promise?"

"Of course. It is not my business, is it? I cannot help but be angry with you, Christine, but it is between you and him. I'll not interfere." He sighed heavily and stood looking down at her, the disapproval clear on his face. "I cannot speak for James, of course. He will most definitely want to interfere."

He went inside the house and she followed, but stayed in the great hall while he went into the smaller room to talk to Michael.

Her own image presided over the huge fireplace, a full length, life sized painting of her on her wedding day, in that beautiful gown Michael had ordered specially. She barely recognised herself. Her painted smile was joyful, forcing her to recall the happiness she had felt the day this was painted. It was the week after the wedding that the artist finished the painting, having started his preparations and sketches weeks before. By the time it was completed, she was hopelessly in love with Michael and it showed in that smile.

She recalled how she had wanted to thank her father for arranging this match, but she knew her happiness and the goodness of her new husband was mere coincidence. She had been fortunate, nothing more. The angels had smiled on her, but the angels were deceitful; they had turned their backs on her when she needed them, just as Michael had.

She waited with her heart hammering, trying to summon the courage to wait and face him. She had never known him to be angry, except where Edmund Carstairs was concerned; but his anger was almost uncontrollable on that one day when he had seen Edmund holding her, seen him kissing her and thought she was a willing partner to the embrace. He had called her a whore, had called her his leftovers and that had hurt so much she wanted to run after him and hit him with something. Had Edmund not kept a firm grip on her, she would have done so.

She had called after him, tried to make him listen, but he just climbed on his horse and rode away, back to London, leaving her to fend for herself.

Would he still be angry, still think her a whore? He would think it even more when he saw her figure. She was not prepared for that sort of heartache but she could not flee; there was nowhere to go.

***

His two elder brothers were still debating, still arguing about Christine when John slipped into the room and closed the door behind him. He did not want her to hear her husband's reaction to the news, not in her condition. Were it not for that condition, he would not care. The woman had betrayed his brother and she deserved no special consideration from him. Were it not for Michael's devotion to her, he would have been happy to leave her perched on the cliff top.

"Michael," he began. "I have to speak to you."

He wanted to speak to him alone, but he had left Christine on the other side of that door and he had no wish for James to leave and find her first. There was no telling what he would do.

"Not now, John," Michael replied, pushing himself to his feet. He picked up his hat and cloak, swung the latter around his shoulders. "I have to go before I lose the will. It is going to be hard enough without leaving time to think on it."

"This is important."

"Did you not hear your brother?" James interrupted. "He has a difficult task to perform."

John took a deep breath as Michael came toward him. His fists clenched but he made no move away from the door, just stood blocking the way.

"Please, John. Get out of my way. I need to do this."

"Perhaps not," John said.

"What does that mean, exactly?"

Michael was growing angry now, it was apparent from his flushed face and harsh tone.

"It means, Michael, that I have brought someone to see you."

Michael scowled.

"I have no time for visitors, John. I need to find my wife."

"It is your wife."

Michael stood still and stared at his younger brother. It was evident he was shocked, thought perhaps he had misheard and could find no words. His eyes moved past John, as though he might see through the solid oak, but the door was firmly closed and he could see nothing. He looked back at John.

"Christine?" He murmured.

"She is here?" James demanded, jumping to his feet. "The whore has the nerve to show her face uninvited."

"She was invited," John told him. "I invited her."

James moved to the door, but John was not about to let him get to her first. At that moment, Michael seemed to gather some composure and he turned to James.

"No, you will not go to her. I will go to her."

He began to move to the door again, but John put out a hand to rest on his brother's chest and halt his steps.

"There is something you should know before you see her. She is with child."

Michael was shaking his head now, tears sprang to his eyes and he clung onto his brother, gripping both his arms as he half fell forward.

"It is true, Michael. I am sorry."

"That is it!" This from James. "She is not welcome in this house! I do not care who invited her!"

He tried to force his way past his brothers to grip the door knob, and it was obvious he intended to throw Christine out of the house, even though it was not his place.

Michael drew himself up to his full height, swallowed and spoke.

"She is still my wife, James, still Countess of Melford. I will hear what she has to say."

***

Christine heard raised voices from the next room, but the door was firmly closed so she could not hear what was being said, or even whose voice it was. She hoped it was not Michael's, but she had no way of knowing and as she waited, the urge to escape was growing more powerful by the minute.

She wanted to run away. Were it not for the precious cargo within her womb, she would have run away, but this unborn child was her reason for being here. She had nowhere to go and she would not risk the safety of her baby by returning to the cliff side cottage.

Still angry from the humiliation she had suffered, she needed Michael whether he wanted to help her or not; she had no choice. Were it not for John finding her, she would have been forced to come here long before this.

The argument continued as she stared at her portrait and wondered why it still hung here, presiding over the great hall. Christine had seen no mirrors for months, but she was quite sure she looked nothing like the beauty in that painting.

Looking down at her own wrist, she noticed for the first time how thin that wrist had become, how her skin only barely hid the bone. She was surprised John had even recognised her.

When she heard the door open, she took an involuntary step towards the main doors, then stopped and listened to the footfalls as they came rapidly closer behind her. She could sense his presence, knew it was her husband, and her eyes filled with more of those tears of despair. She had shed more tears these last few months than in her whole lifetime put together and she blamed Michael for those tears.

"Christine?"

She turned slowly, stared up at him and her heart skipped to see his handsome face once more. She watched his eyes sweep her figure, watched the downward turn of his mouth, watched him bite down on his lip, those lips which had always smiled so warmly for her.

"Michael," she answered, keeping her position.

She would go no closer; she would not trust herself to go closer. She might bunch up her fists and hit him or she might throw her arms around him; she had no idea which.

For a long moment it seemed that time stood still as they stared at each other, neither one wanting to be the first to move, to speak. She fought hard to cling to her anger at Michael, for leaving her when she needed him, but all she really wanted to do was to hold him in her arms again, to feel his lips on hers again. At last she could stand it no longer.

"Michael," she said, cradling her stomach. "This child is yours. It has a right to a place in this house."

A smile tried to force its way onto his lips, but he pushed it back. It had not been there long enough for her to know if it were a smile of joy or one of mockery, she thought the latter.

"How do you know it is mine?" He demanded.

The tears spilled over then, she could hold them back no longer but they were tears of frustration as much as anything. To relieve that frustration, she slapped his face, hard, leaving an angry red mark on his beardless cheek.

He gasped in shock, his hand going to his injured face, but instead of being angry, his heart melted. He should not have said that.

"Forgive me," he murmured.

He stepped toward her and pulled her into his arms, felt the flutter against his body as he kissed her face.

"It could be no one else's child, Michael," she mumbled against his chest. "Had you listened to me instead of letting your jealousy chase away common sense, you would have known that."

Were it not for the child, she would never have seen Michael again. She was angry and hurt, disappointed with his reaction, and she had come here determined to keep her distance. But feeling his warmth, feeling his arms around her again almost destroyed her resolve.

He led her to a bench at the table and went to the cabinet to pour her some wine, then sat beside her while she drank.

"Thank you," she said, putting the goblet down on the table.

It had been a long time since she tasted fine wine. She turned to face him, her eyes meeting his through the blur of her tears and was relieved to finally see that familiar warm smile.

He took her hand in his, another familiar gesture she had missed so much. Why did he do that, when she wanted to stay angry with him?

"Christine," he said. "I have missed you so much. I came back here in the spring, hoping to find you, but you had left. It has been torture for me, living without you, sleeping in that empty bed without you beside me. I want you to come back to me. Whatever happened, whatever you have done, I will forgive you."

The words churned up her fury once more and she snatched her hand away, tilted the goblet to her lips and drained it then slammed it down on the table. She jumped to her feet and stared down at him where he still sat at the table.

"Forgive me, will you?" She demanded, her voice rising. "That is very generous of you. I have been abducted by a madman, been forced to suffer his hands on me, been torn away from my baby and frightened out of my senses, and you would forgive me?"

She was so angry she almost slapped him again.

"Christine, what are you telling me?"

"Do you not see, Michael?" She said harshly. "I am not sure I can ever forgive you."

Michael made no reply but he got up and moved back, put some distance between them. Christine had never shown anger before, not to him. She was always gentle and placid, which is why they suited each other so well. Now she sounded like she wanted to scream at him.

He wore a puzzled frown and his cheeks flushed, his jaw clenched and she could see he was trying to understand her words. She would not enlighten him; let him think about it.

Christine could scarcely believe she was in Melford Hall, her husband beside her. She closed her eyes and tried to convince herself that she was still in the draughty cottage on the clifftop, or the empty Manor House, but when she opened them again it was all real. Now all she had to do was keep it.

"What are you saying, Christine?" He asked again.

She noticed the quiver of his lip and reached up a hand to stroke his face, to comfort him, but she snatched it away. What was she doing? She wanted to be angry with him, not soothing his sorrow. What about her sorrow?

"May I go to my chamber, please," she said.

"Of course. It is still your chamber; it always will be."

His eyes dropped down to her swollen figure.

"When is...the baby?"

"A few more weeks."

"I shall send for a midwife; she will be able to give a more precise date, unless you..."

He did not have to finish the question. Christine knew what he was going to ask, unless she knew precisely when it was due because she would know the precise time it was conceived.

She stood rigidly, that anger consuming her again.

"Yes, Michael," she said bitterly. "You send for a midwife to examine me and when she tells you this child was conceived at Yuletide, in London, you can start to wonder when Edmund could have sneaked into your London house. Or you could take my word that it is your child."

"Then you were living with him, while carrying my child?"

"If you like. It rather depends on what you mean by living with him, does it not?"

"You know what I mean."

His voice had risen, his face darkened and he stepped away from her.

"Yes, I know what you mean. Michael, no man has ever touched me, no man but you." She paused and drew a breath, tried in vain not to voice the next words. "Of course, had I not shifted for myself and got away, had I relied on your protection, I might not be able to tell you that."

"I saw you kissing him."

"No!" She shouted in his face, her own anger growing into rage with the frustration of his disbelief. "You saw him kissing me. You saw him forcing me to stay in his embrace while he pushed his wet lips onto mine and that is all you saw before you left, leaving me with my abductor."

Michael was shaking his head.

"You came down here to meet him."

"I came down here to be godmother to Joan's baby, as I promised. Now she thinks I broke my promise to her so I could run off with a lover. I daresay the whole town, the whole county believes me a faithless whore. I doubt you and your brothers have done anything to dissuade them. But I care nothing for their opinions, only for yours."

"Your abductor?" He whispered.

She nodded, searching his eyes for some sign of acceptance.

"He told me you loved him, that you wanted to marry him until I came along and tore you away from him."

Of course, that must have been when Edmund came here, just after Lisa's birth. She knew nothing about his earlier visit, just after their marriage. Michael had never told her about that. She had insisted on seeing him, she had even insisted on seeing him alone because she was angry that Michael did not trust her. She wanted only to tell him to stay away, that she loved Michael and that is what she had told him.

After seeing the delusional way he ignored her protests during that awful day he had kept her prisoner in his house, she now realised her words had meant nothing. He must have waited for Michael and told him his lies. And Michael had believed them.

"He lied," she said. "Why did you believe him? Why did you not ask me if it were true?"

"Because I was afraid of the answer."

She shook her head, her mouth wearing a line of bitterness, and the heartache in her voice as she spoke almost tore him apart.

"Why did you not fight for me?"

***

John leaned his full weight against the heavy oak door, his arms folded as he resisted James' attempts to push him out of the way.

"How dare you?" James yelled. "Get out of my way, John, or so help me I'll not be responsible."

"No. I brought Christine here and I am not going to allow you to frighten her away. Leave them alone, please. They need to talk."

"I have some talking to do to that trollop myself!"

James put his full weight behind his push, but John would not budge.

"It is not your business," John answered. "Can you not see that?"

"What I see is that Michael will take her back, disgrace the whole family. He'll not even order any punishment for her adultery; without my guidance he will allow her to manipulate him again. And what of the brat? What will he do with that when it is born, send it back to its father? Or allow her to keep it under his roof?"

"Whatever he decides is not our business, James. It is between Michael and his wife."

"As long as my family live in this house it is my business."

John stepped forward, wanting to embrace his brother and perhaps make him see Michael's point of view, but it was a mistake. James took the opportunity to shove him out of the way and escape into the great hall, where Michael stood with his wife, being reasonable as usual.

"Why did you not fight for me?"

Those were the words James heard as he came through the door.

"Fight?" He yelled. "For you? Was that your plan, for my brother to shed blood on your behalf?"

Michael turned toward him and scowled.

"James, go away. This is between me and my wife."

"Wife? I think she has forfeited the right to that title. What happened? Did Carstairs tire of you? Did he throw you out now you are swollen and of no further use to him?"

"James! You will not speak to my wife like that."

"So you have decided then to take her back. I might have known."

"Nothing has yet been decided, James. Christine and I have a lot to talk about before anything can be determined. Whatever happens, it is not your concern. Stay out of it, please."

The quarrel the brothers were having only caused Christine more grief. She did not need this, did she? She had never liked James, thought him a bully like her father, and while she knew that Michael would not allow him to influence his decision, she could not bear this. She wanted to leave, to go back to the Manor House where she could at least be free from all this controversy and confrontation.

"Perhaps I could go to the Manor House?" Christine asked quietly. "Nobody wants me here, nobody wants to listen. I would be better there."

"I want you here," said Michael. "Your place is with me."

"I will tell you one thing now, Michael," James shouted, his finger waving angrily at Christine. "I do not want that whore anywhere near my wife. I do not want her under the same roof as Helen."

Michael spun around. That temper was slow to ignite, it always had been, but now he strode towards James, his teeth clenched, his hands bunched into fists and his brother could almost feel the bruise to his jaw.

"Then you had best remove Helen and yourself. The manor house stands empty; make use of it."

CHAPTER SEVEN

Michael watched his wife climb the staircase to her bedchamber, the one that had stood empty since last autumn when they all moved to London. He had gone there often since their return in the spring, just wandering around the chamber and touching her things, breathing in the lingering smell of her perfume. He turned his gaze to rest on his brother, James.

"You mean it?" James demanded. "You would turn us out for her?"

Michael sighed heavily. All he wanted was for James to go and leave him to talk with Christine in peace. He was still trying to convince himself that she was really here, that he had not fallen asleep and dreamed it. And he desperately needed to think about her words. Was she right? Had he made the most horrendous mistake? Had he left her to fend for herself against a lunatic who would imprison her and force himself on her? Had he let his jealousy make his decisions for him? If he had, if she spoke the truth, how would he ever make it up to her?

At last he turned back to James.

"Your occupation of this house was always supposed to be temporary, James," he said. "You know that. The Manor House was renovated for your use; it is high time you took your wife and your sons and moved into it."

"Very well, but be assured, your attitude will not be easily forgotten."

"Nor will yours. James, I have tolerated your insults to my wife long enough; now she is back and I would like to persuade her to stay." He paused and held up his hand as James opened his mouth to argue. "I know, I do not need to persuade her. She is my wife; she should do as I tell her. But I do not want her to stay unless it is what she wants. Take some of the servants, take some supplies and leave, please."

"You are a fool, Michael. Others might believe your temperament to be placid and gentle; I believe it to be weak."

Michael made no reply, only watched as James went in search of his own wife. When he was out of earshot, he turned his attention to his younger brother who had followed James into the hall and now stood quietly, watching, listening. His expression gave nothing away, but Michael was sure he found James' blustering quite amusing. He would find it so himself were circumstances different.

He was grateful to John; at first he had believed he had taken it upon himself to ride to Carstairs Manor and retrieve Christine, to spare him the humiliation. He was just now realising he had not been gone long enough.

"Where did you find her?" He asked.

John drew a decisive breath.

"In the old fisherman's cottage on the cliff top."

Michael's eyes widened.

"What on earth made you think to look there?"

"I was not looking, Michael," John said hesitantly. "I found her there months ago, in the spring, quite by chance. I took her to the Manor House, made her more comfortable there."

Michael stared silently at his brother, his mind trying very hard to process this information and that unfamiliar anger began to rise again.

"And she has been there all this time?" He demanded. "Less than a mile away?"

John nodded, cast his eyes at his feet.

"Why did you not tell me?"

"She asked me not to. She made me promise, Michael."

"All the time I have been in torment, thinking of her living with Carstairs, enjoying his favours, and you knew she was here, on my own land? Yet you said nothing? Why?"

"Had it just been Christine, I would have told you, I swear, no matter what she wanted. But there was the babe. I could not bear for you to know about the babe. Were it not for Grace's wedding and your determination to bring her back, I would not have told you even now. I would have found somewhere else for her to stay until all the guests had gone."

"You would have kept us apart?" Michael shouted. "How dare you? What right do you have to interfere like that?"

"I wanted only what was best for you, Michael. I did not want to see you hurt again."

"That was not your decision to make."

"Perhaps not, but I thought you deserved better. I wanted you to get over her, perhaps even divorce her and wed again. I thought only to protect you."

Michael scowled, his complexion darkened. He was furious now, but more with himself than his brothers. They both thought themselves qualified to interfere in his life, for his own good. Were he like James, nobody would be thinking of protecting him, would they? But he could never be like him and he was not sorry, even if it had lost him the love of his life.

What had she said? Why had he not fought for her? Did she invite Carstairs to her bedchamber just to make him jealous, to see if he would be prepared to fight him? He shook his head as that little spark of hope died. No, that could not be it. She had no idea he would follow her here, did she? So what had she meant? He was not sure he understood his own question, but it was time to find out.

He left John seated in the great hall and mounted the staircase, strode along the gallery to Christine's chamber, but he stopped when he heard murmured voices. The door stood ajar and he peeped inside to see his wife seated on the bed, his sister in her arms; both were weeping.

"Christine, I knew you would not have gone without telling me," Grace was mumbling through her tears. "Not without even saying goodbye."

"I am glad you realised that, darling," Christine was saying. "I wish Michael had also realised it."

"He is a fool! I could see you loved him; why could he not see it too?"

Christine held Grace at arm's length and smiled haltingly.

"Because he is a man," she said. "A jealous man who failed to see he had nothing whatever of which to be jealous. Your Jason, do you love him?"

Grace swept the back of her hand over her eyes to wipe away the tears and swallowed hard before she answered.

"Not yet," she said. "But I will. He is very nice, very amiable. Michael went to a lot of effort to be sure of my happiness, so I expect nothing less. If only he had made the same effort on his own behalf, we would all be better off."

"Is my Lisa well?"

Grace jumped to her feet.

"She is; she is adorable. She started to walk this summer..." She stopped talking abruptly and blushed. "Forgive me. You do not want to hear about what you have missed."

"Is she sleeping? If not, I will see her now."

Michael had heard enough. He bit back a catch in his voice to interrupt them.

"As soon as she awakes, I will bring her to you," he said as he walked into the chamber. "Grace, will you give us some time, please."

She leaned forward and kissed Christine, then turned and moved toward the door, stopping before her brother.

"I hope you know what an idiot you are," she muttered.

They both watched her go, watched her close the door behind her, then Michael sat beside his wife and took her hand.

"What did you mean, about not being able to forgive me?"

She made no reply for a moment, her eyes meeting his as she tried to stop herself from hitting him, while at the same time stopping herself from throwing her arms around him. He must deserve one or the other, but she could not decide which.

"You really have no idea, do you?"

Michael frowned and shook his head. She was right; he really did have no idea and he could not believe she had contrived the situation with Carstairs just to see if he would fight for her. Christine would never do something like that, he was sure, so what on earth was she talking about? What had he done for which he might need her forgiveness?

"Tell me, please," Michael said, holding tight to her hand.

Christine bit her lips to keep them from creasing up. He had had all these months to consider what he had seen, to think about their time together and realise she was in love with him, not some other man. He had had all these months to try to find her, but he had done nothing.

She was angry with him; she wanted to stay angry with him, but it was not easy. He had let her go because he believed that was what she wanted. How could she be angry about that?

"Michael, I came down here in the spring to stand as godmother to Joan's baby, just as I promised her. Do you really believe I would have broken that promise? Do you think I would have let her down, when I knew how much it meant to her?"

He was thoughtful for a moment.

"I suppose not. I thought it was your only chance to escape with him; I never considered that you would be breaking your promise to a tenant. It never really occurred to me."

"No, it did not, did it? Yet that alone should have told you I was being abducted, taken away against my will."

Michael released her hand and moved just a little way along the bed from her. He was slowly shaking his head, his mouth turned down.

"I saw you in his arms; I saw you kissing him."

"No, Michael. You saw him kissing me. You saw him holding me in his arms and were you not so eaten up with jealousy, you would have seen my struggle to release myself. When he let go of me I called to you to come back; you ignored me." She paused, the anger welling up again. "No, you did worse than ignore me. You called me a whore; you called me your leftovers."

Tears sprang to her eyes and began to brim over; she wiped at them with her fingers, but more poured down.

"I am sorry, Christine," he said, taking her hand again. "I meant none of that. I was angry."

"Yes, you were angry. Likely, for the first time in your life you were angry, but instead of being angry with him, you decided to direct that anger at me. Do you have any idea how much those words of yours hurt? Can you even imagine how it felt, knowing I was in danger from Edmund, while my husband was standing only a few feet away and would not help me?"

Michael frowned, disbelief still clear in his blue eyes.

"You are saying I let you down," he said. "When you needed me, I walked away from you."

"Yes, you let me down! You allowed that madman to take me away from you, from our daughter. Why would you think I would leave Lisa? Or Grace? It showed me what you really thought about me, despite your endearments. Your declarations of love meant nothing."

"No, Christine. I love you; I always have."

She shook her head.

"No, Michael. If you loved me you would have killed Edmund before you gave in to him."

"It was because I loved you I let you go."

"He took me to Carstairs Manor," Christine went on. "He forced me into his carriage and he took me to his house. He even convinced the coachman that I was his wife who had run away from him. He had it all prepared as though it were our wedding feast and he dragged me up the stairs. I was so frightened, so afraid to let him know about this child lest he hurt it." As she spoke she cradled her swollen womb, rested her hands protectively over the new life her husband did not believe he had put there. "He would have raped me, Michael. And where were you? Nursing a broken heart of your own making."

CHAPTER EIGHT

While Michael wanted more than anything to believe what his wife was telling him, because that would mean she had never loved Carstairs, he was afraid to consider it. She was telling him he was wrong, that he had spent these months missing her, believing her to be with another man, suffering such hurt and jealousy for no reason at all. It would mean she had remained faithful to him, that the child she carried was indeed his own. But if he believed that, he had to believe he had abandoned her when she needed him most, when she was in danger of being violated by that man.

He did not want to think about that, but which was worse? If she did really love him, had he destroyed that love? Had he put himself and her through months of heartache and loneliness because he could never accept that such an angel could really love him?

"If he took you to Carstairs Manor, where was his father? Where was his brother?"

She laughed, a bitter laugh he could not interpret.

"His father died last yuletide," she said. "He killed Roger so that he could have the estate, because he thought that was all he needed to also have me."

Did he believe that? He was not sure, but it would be easy enough to find out if Roger, too was dead.

"When he realised I would not give in to him, he got it into his head that it was because you stood between us. He was going to kill you, too, Michael. I had to pretend to really want him, so he would not try to kill you."

"How did you get away?"

"I climbed out of the window and down an oak tree."

He grinned a little, which he had not intended to do. It seemed very unlikely that a lady of Christine's class, with child, would be climbing out of windows and down trees. She pulled up her skirts to show him her legs, to show him the healed white scars where she had scraped her shins on the tree bark.

She turned to show him a cynical grimace.

"Of course, I could be lying," she said.

"I never said you were lying."

"You did not have to. Why was it so easy for you to believe I wanted another man?" She demanded. "Did I not tell you that I loved you? Did I not love you enough, did I not show my desire for you? Was I not passionate enough for you?"

He tried to speak, but the words could not get past the ache in his throat. He swallowed, still unsure of what he believed or what he should say.

"I knew you had been seeing him before I asked for your hand," he said. "Your father told me he was pleased with my petition because it would separate you from him."

"There was never anything between us. That was my father's idea and, apparently, Edmund's too. You never asked me how I felt." She caught back a sob. "Nobody ever asked me how I felt."

"Twice I found him here; that first time he came, I said nothing but the next time, you insisted on seeing him." He paused and frowned at her. "Why did you insist on seeing him?"

"So I could tell him I never wanted to see him again. So he would leave us alone."

"Really? I thought, perhaps..." He sighed, then went on: "Then I found him again a little while later, lurking about the stable yard. He ran off when he saw me that time, but the other times he told me you had been committed to him, that you loved him."

"And you believed him? You did not even bother to ask me."

No, he did not ask her, but it had nothing to do with not bothering. It was because he was afraid of the answer, afraid she might confirm Carstairs' story. He wanted to protect himself when he should have been protecting her.

The shame almost consumed him and he turned away to hide his face from her before he spoke again. She said nothing, but he could feel her trembling, could feel the vibrations from her sobs.

"Christine, I felt guilty," he said at last, turning back to her. "He was very convincing and I thought about how I had asked for you like I asked for an architect to design this house. When I suddenly became Earl, the first thing I thought was that I could have the house I wanted after all, and the beautiful stallion I had my eye on and I could also have you. I was not treating you as an intelligent human being, but as a piece of property like my horse. When I realised that, it seemed likely I had torn you away from your real love. I just wanted you to be happy; I thought I would make you happy by letting you go to him."

Months of regret welled up inside him until he could think of nothing else. Had he really thrown away everything they had? Had he really allowed his jealousy to govern his actions and put her through worry and isolation? How was he ever going to make this up to her?

He put his arm around her, pulled her close to him, allowed his warm hand to caress her neck and kissed her with all the passion he had held inside while he was missing her. For the first time she made no attempt to return his kiss.

He released her, but took her face in his hands. His eyes met hers for a moment, then he pulled her into his arms and held her close, kissed her forehead and hugged her.

"You really cannot forgive me, can you?" He said.

She swiped at more of those treacherous tears.

"I am not sure, Michael. This child I carry is yours and I do not think you believe that. Until you do, the answer is no, I cannot forgive you."

He made no reply. There seemed to be nothing more he could say, not now. His mind was a whirl of indecision and distrust; what was he to think? He would give the world to know that Christine loved him, not Carstairs, but he was not sure he could carry the shame of letting her down so badly.

"Can I see my baby now?" She asked him.

"Of course." He got to his feet. "I will ask her nurse to bring her to you. How long before...?" His words halted. He did not want to mention the birth and he realised she was right; he did not accept the child was his.

"It is due in about four weeks time," she replied. "Before the wedding, so I will still be able to see Grace married. If that pleases you, of course."

"Just having you here pleases me. It means the world to me."

"So you say."

***

While she waited, Christine allowed her emotions to dissolve into the tears she had been trying hard to keep inside, with little success. She was so pleased to see Michael again, would be so happy to hold him in her arms, to kiss him, but the resentment refused to step aside and allow her love to show through. She could never forget how frightened she had been, knowing that if she did not escape, Edmund would force himself on her; she could not forget that Michael could have prevented that from ever happening, but he did not.

She stroked her swollen stomach again, felt the child within move vigorously. He doubted her, he did not believe this baby was of his making; no, she could never forgive that, no matter how much she wanted to.

The child the nurse carried into the chamber had grown so much, Christine could scarce believe it. She was expecting a tiny babe, but this child was a little human being and she looked at her mother doubtfully as the nurse approached the bed.

Christine held out her arms and the nurse placed the baby into them. Then she stood and waited, which irritated Christine. Had Michael told the woman to watch her with the baby? Was this another example of his distrust?

"You may go now, Dorothy," she said.

"It is quite all right, My Lady," Dorothy replied. "I have no other duties."

"Then you can use the time to take refreshments or walk in the sunshine."

"No, My Lady. I am perfectly all right."

Christine's temper flared. She had suffered for months, been lonely for months with only John for occasional company, a man whose goodwill was denied her. She did not need the insolence of this woman and she would not tolerate it.

"Dorothy, you misunderstand. I told you to go. I wish to spend time with my daughter."

The nurse shuffled her feet uncomfortably.

"I will ask His Lordship," she said.

The venom in Christine's glare should have told the nurse she had gone too far, but still she made no move to leave.

"Not if you value your position," Christine said, her voice rising. "Now get out, before I throw you out!"

A sudden dart of pain shot through her heart when she watched the nurse leave and little Lisa put out her arms to her retreating figure. The child had no idea who she was, her own mother, and whose fault was that?

The door opened and she looked up sharply, expecting to see that Dorothy had returned. The woman must be made to know her place or Christine would not allow her to stay in her employ.

But it was Helen's pretty face which peered into the chamber, her smile one of delight and Christine was so pleased to see a friend.

"May I come in?" She asked.

"Of course you may. Please, close the door and come and sit beside me."

Helen accepted the invitation and sat on the bed, stroked little Lisa's smooth cheek and leaned forward to kiss her. The little girl giggled happily.

"She is pleased to see a friendly face," Christine said. "I am a stranger to her."

"Not for long, I am sure. Children soon forget, soon become accustomed to a change in their surroundings." She paused and reached out to take Christine's hand in her own. "I am so happy to see you," she said.

"I take it James does not know you are here."

"He is off buying more furniture for the guest rooms at the Manor House. There will be a lot of people staying with us for the wedding and he wants to make it homely."

"What will he do if he finds out?"

"He will talk," Helen answered with a smile. "He will threaten, he will disapprove."

"What else?"

"Nothing else," Helen said. "He makes a lot of noise, but he would never lay a hand on me. It is not in his nature, believe me. He is not as different from his brother as he would like to pretend."

"He thinks I am a bad influence on you."

"Of course he does, but I make up my own mind about things and he knows it, really. I only pretend to involve him in my decisions because it pleases him."

Christine shook her head in astonishment.

"Why do you do that?"

"Because I love him," she said. "And because I need him. He loves me too, although he is too proud to admit it."

"Oh, Helen," Christine said. "I used to think you were the unfortunate one, that your husband ordered your every move. But if James believed you were in love with another man, he would have killed him and dragged you home, kicking and screaming if necessary."

"He would, yes."

"Which is worse? Michael did not fight for me; he thought he was letting me go to the man I loved, and now I have to convince him that this child I carry is of his own making."

They sat in silence for a few moments, Christine thinking about her own words and wondering how she would ever repair the damage, wondering why it should fall to her to make those repairs. Helen looked wary, as though not sure if she should voice her question.

"What happened, Christine?" She asked at last. "All I know is what the men have told me. Michael says you came down here before the rest of the family to meet with Edmund Carstairs, that you ran away with him."

"What do you say, Helen?" She asked. "Do you think I would leave my baby? Do you think me such a whore as to leave my husband, run away with another man?"

"No, Christine, I do not. I never did; I could see you loved Michael, even if he failed to see it himself. Either that, or your acting skills are excellent."

"I came here to stand as godmother to the child of one of the tenants, as I promised her. Edmund was waiting for me. He must have been watching the house, waiting for the family to start returning from London."

"So you did not come to meet him?"

"Of course not! I came for Joan, as I said. I came into this chamber to change after my journey and he followed me. I did not think to lock the front doors and there were no servants about, no one to help me."

Tears welled up and her mouth turned down as she remembered that awful day.

"He grabbed me, pushed his wet lips onto me, even shoved his disgusting tongue into my mouth and I tried to push him away. I told him I did not want him, that I loved my husband, but he refused to listen. He said Michael had put those ideas into my head, as though I was too stupid to know my own mind."

Helen put her arms around Christine and hugged her, trying to soothe the tears which continued to flow.

"I wish I could stop crying," she muttered, wiping her face on her sleeve.

Helen reached into her own sleeve and handed her a cloth.

"It is over now," she murmured.

"No, it is not over. He killed his brother, Helen."

Helen gasped.

"Are you sure?"

"Yes, he told me. He was proud of it, said he did it for me, so that we could be together. He thought we would be sharing a bed; when I refused he threatened to kill Michael. He is insane. I persuaded him to wait until the following night, made him promise not to hurt Michael, and I escaped. I walked back here; I was exhausted and I ached all over, but when I got here, there he was, sitting on the steps waiting for me."

"Oh, my God!"

"I had nowhere to go. There were workmen at the Manor House still and I was so tired, I just had to rest. I found shelter in the old fisherman's cottage on the cliff."

"What? That place is derelict, not fit to house the rats."

"It is not so bad. The weather was improving and I managed to buy some supplies in the village with the money I still had. Nobody recognised me, thank goodness, probably because of the way I was dressed. I just grabbed a woollen blanket when I escaped from Carstairs Manor. I thought I would be less conspicuous. I must have looked like a peasant, which was just as well. I knew the family would be coming home in a few weeks or so, but John came down here first for some reason. I never have asked him why."

"And he found you? Why did he not say anything?"

"The same reason I had decided by then I did not want Michael to know where I was until I had time to decide how to persuade him that I carry his child. John did not want him to know about the baby, because he is sure it is Edmund's."

"He left you there?"

"No. He assured me that the workmen had finished and that James had not yet taken up residence in the Manor House. I have been staying there and he has been bringing me supplies. I knew I would have to appeal to Michael eventually, but I hoped he might see the truth for himself before then. Obviously, I was wrong."

Baby Lisa reached out her arms to Helen, who gave her a finger to squeeze. She could see the child wanted to be held by her, but she made no move to take her from her mother. Christine needed this time with her, needed the baby to learn to know her again.

"What will you do?" Helen asked. "Michael has been so unhappy without you."

Christine shrugged, her mouth forming a line of bitterness.

"He brought that on himself," she said. "I love him, Helen. I have always loved him, but I should have been here, in the comfort of my own home, sharing the joy of this new baby with its father. I have been denied those things because of his reluctance to challenge Edmund."

"He thought it was what you wanted."

"I know what he thought. If I thought otherwise I would not be here. I would have persuaded John to sell something so I could get away. But the fact is, he believed I would leave him, he believed I would betray him and he has not accepted this child as his own. Until he does, I cannot think about a future for us."

CHAPTER NINE

Christine was resting the following day when Michael entered the chamber, came to sit on the bed and kissed her gently. She wanted to return his kiss, she wanted to hold him close to her and rekindle the love they once had, but she was still too disappointed. She tried to be angry, but she could not hold on to that anger, not when Michael was so attentive, so loving.

"Christine," he said. "I have brought the Constable from Colchester. I know it is not customary for him to see you in your condition, but I believe we need to start investigations against Carstairs as quickly as possible. Do you mind seeing him?"

Immediately she suspected his motives. She could not help it.

"You want me to bring charges against Edmund for abducting me?" She demanded. "Is that to prove the truth of it?"

Shock showed on Michael's face, making her want to snatch back the words.

"No," he said. "It is because he abducted my wife, held her against her will and is quite likely to return. Will you feel comfortable with that? Will you feel safe, riding out alone? I recall how you always loved to ride along the beach alone."

Michael was right and it had not even occurred to her. The way Edmund was behaving, as though he knew best no matter what she said, she would not be safe, would she? Coming home was only the beginning and she should have done so months ago, when the family first arrived here for the summer. She had let pride stop her and now people would wonder why she had left it so long.

"Forgive me," she murmured. "Of course he must be arrested."

"And you told me he killed his brother. Do you think he should be allowed to escape justice for that?"

Michael's voice had risen in irritation and now she stared at him, trying to fathom his reasons for that ire. He believed she did not want Edmund arrested, that she did not want him to pay for his crimes. He would be hanged and Michael believed she was against that. In truth she was unsure how she felt about that. She had known Edmund for many years, always thought of him as a friend. Did she really want to be the cause of his execution?

But she would not be the cause, would she? He brought that on himself when he decided to do away with his own brother. And he had chosen a very cowardly means to dispose of Roger; poison, a woman's weapon. He did not even have the courage to fight him, to face him like a man. He had terrified her, threatened her husband, separated her from her baby, ruined her happiness – why should she feel any reluctance to help him to his just penalty?

She sighed heavily. How were they ever to rebuild their lives if he suspected her every gesture, if she suspected his?

"Of course I will see the Constable," she said at last. "And you must stay to hear my statement, else you might believe I want to protect my abductor."

"No," he argued.

"Yes. I can see how your mind is working; I can tell that you think I want him spared."

She shook her head and those tears leapt to her eyes again, but she steeled herself. She would not give in to those tears, not this time. She would bite down on her creasing lips and show him that he was not hurting her, when all she wanted was to melt into the arms of the man she missed so much.

Michael picked up her velvet cloak and swept it about her shoulders, closed both sides to cover her figure and gestured to the Constable to approach and sit in the chair beside the bed.

"My Lady," he said respectfully. "I shall be brief. You must tell me all that happened and why it has taken you so long to report the crime."

Christine glanced at Michael in alarm, then her eyes moved back to the Constable. He did not believe her; he thought it was a ruse she had invented to explain her absence, to fool her husband into believing she had not committed adultery.

"I could not come here immediately," she said. "I escaped from Mr Carstairs' house and I walked here." The constable raised an eyebrows, his scepticism clear. "When I arrived, he was here, waiting for me. I had many reasons not to show myself after that, all of which are personal and nothing to do with you."

"Well, My Lady, if you wish to press charges, I have to know your reasons."

That was enough to release the pent up emotions. Her lips creased, her tears flowed and she turned away.

Michael stood to lead the man out, but he made no move to leave his chair, only turned back to Christine.

"My Lady, if nothing can be learned about Lord Carstairs' death, you will have to give evidence in court. Are you prepared for that?"

"Yes, I realise that. What are you insinuating?"

"I only want you to know that perjury carries a hefty prison sentence."

It was the final straw; she could take no more insults, she who had done nothing but try her best to escape a madman.

"Get out!" She cried. "Just go will you? I will give evidence, yes. He told me he killed Roger for us, because he wanted the wealth for me. The fact that I did not want him seemed to be something he could not accept and he would have raped me had I not escaped."

She turned away and buried her head in the pillow.

The Constable took a deep breath.

"As long as you realise, My Lady," he said.

"I think that is enough," Michael said. "You have been told what happened; now go, do your duty and arrest the man."

Christine heard Michael call for a servant to escort the Constable outside, she heard the door close and felt Michael's weight as he returned to the bed. He reached out and touched her shoulder gently and she raised her head to look at him through blurred vision, her tear stained face wet and puffy.

He pulled her into his arms, kissed her face, drew a cloth from the drawer and wiped her face.

"He does not believe me either," she said angrily.

"Either?"

"You do not believe me. Were it not for John's word that he found me in the spring, you would also believe I had been living happily with my lover. You do not believe the child I carry is of your own making. If you do not believe me, how will the Constable, the Justice of the Peace or anyone else?"

"Darling, please, give the man a chance."

"Why? It is obvious his mind is made up, just as yours is. Edmund really believed I wanted to be with him, that I loved him. He believed I was pried away from him, that I wanted to marry him, not you. That is what he will tell the Constable when he goes there and that is what he will believe."

"Why should he?"

"Because I am a whore in his eyes, just as I am in yours."

"No, Christine, please. I would never think that of you."

"No? That is what you called me."

She turned away to stare out of the window at the meadows and the scattered cottages, at the sea on the horizon, grey today and she imagined cold. She could not bear to look at him.

"I was angry, Christine," he said. He touched her arm, hoping to turn her to face him but she shrugged him off. "I did not mean it; you know I did not mean it."

"You said it, so you must have thought it. Anyway, what else would you call it? You believe I was unfaithful to you; if I was, that would make me a whore. I see no other word for it."

Michael held her close and she so wanted to hold him in return, so wanted to feel his lips on hers again, to feel that need for him she always knew before. But it was spoilt now and all she could do was try to make him see the truth.

Perhaps they could get past this, perhaps they could recapture what they once had; she wanted that so much, but it would never happen until she knew he believed her.

That was when the baby moved, kicked out at the wall of her womb and touched its father, but its father moved away. He had no idea his involuntary retreat had shattered the future she was considering.

"You see?" Christine said, struggling with more of those damned tears. "You cannot bear to be near it, can you? Do you remember when I carried Lisa, how you would love to put your hand on me and feel her movements, how you would smile as those movements tickled your palm?"

"Of course I do," he answered.

"But not this child, eh, Michael? You do not want to feel the life in this child. I expect you even hope it will not survive the birth, then you will not have to think about it."

"No, Christine! How can you think such a thing?" He reached out again to hold her, but she jumped to her feet and slapped his hands away. "Leave me, please," she said. "Just go. The longer you stay, the more I want to slap you."

Then she cried out, clutched at the bulge of her stomach and stared at him in horror as his eyes moved to the puddle rapidly collecting on the floor between her feet.

***

The midwife was there within the hour and in the meantime, Michael called for Lisa's nurse to help his wife, she being the most likely person to know what to do. He slipped the kirtle from Christine's shoulders, stirring a little as memories assaulted him, and helped her into bed.

"You must go, My Lord," the nurse said. "I can manage until the midwife arrives."

"Very well," he said, turning to the bed. "Is that what you want, Christine?"

"Helen," she said. "I want Helen."

Michael looked doubtful. He had not spoken to his brother since their quarrel when Christine returned; he had no wish to speak to him now.

"I am not sure that James..."

"Get Helen!" Christine yelled impatiently. "She is the only one who understands. To hell with James!"

The pains were coming closer together now, much stronger than when she had Lisa. Still Michael did not move.

"It is too early," she said, then she turned blazing eyes on him. "This is what you wanted, is it not? For the child to come before its time and not survive."

"That is not true, Christine," he replied.

"Go," she cried. "Get Helen. I want Helen."

She kept those angry eyes on Michael until he left and sent a servant to the Manor House to fetch Helen. He would not go himself; he was still angry with his brother and did not want a repeat of their argument, not now.

***

Michael waited outside Christine's chamber, just as he had waited for the birth of his little daughter. Only this time his prayers were not for the baby, only for his wife. He had no sense of anticipation for the child to come, no sense of the miracle about to be brought into the world. Try as he might, he could not feel the same about this child and his only prayer was for his wife to come through it safely.

He was so happy to have found her again and he so wanted to believe her assurances, but he was still torn. Her words pounded in his head, her accusation that were it not for John finding her, he would believe she had been living with Carstairs all this time. But why could he not accept her word? He loved her, did he not? He would die for her, gladly. He had decided to find her with the intention of forgiving her, only to find she could not forgive him.

Helen hurried in, bundled up in a velvet cloak despite the warm weather, and passed him without a word on her way to the bedchamber.

She had come then, he thought abstractedly, and wondered if James knew she was here.

"Michael," John said softly, his hand on his brother's shoulder. Michael had not even noticed him enter the chamber. "It could be hours yet. You need to eat something."

"I am not leaving her, John. Tell me, please. Tell me what she said when you found her."

"Nothing really. Just that she did not want you to know where she was. I assumed she was ashamed of herself and so she should be."

Michael gave him an angry glare which made him step back.

"Did she say anything to make you think you were wrong? Did she deny the child was fathered by Carstairs?"

"She told me the child was yours, but I did not believe her. She did not explain anything else to me. She likely thought it none of my concern."

"She said the child was mine?"

"Yes, Michael, she did." John paused and bit his lip thoughtfully, hesitating to speak his mind. "To be honest, I would have left her there had I not known you would never forgive me."

"When she said she did not want me to know where she was, was that before or after you showed your disbelief?"

"After, I suppose. What are you saying?"

"Just that if you did not believe her, she did not expect me to either. I wish you had told me, John. I really do."

"I thought only to save you pain."

Michael jumped to his feet, that unfamiliar anger rising again.

"I am sick to death of everyone thinking they have to protect me! And obviously it was that very weakness which has lost me the dearest woman in the world. I will never get her back, will I?"

"Perhaps that is just as well," the angry voice came from behind him. "I see she is still causing trouble."

Michael spun around to face James.

"What do you want?" He demanded.

"I want my wife," he replied. "I told you Michael, I do not want her anywhere near Christine, yet here you have the damned cheek to send for her."

"Christine wanted her there."

"Christine wanted? Who the hell cares what that trollop wants?"

Michael took one step toward James and was only prevented from hitting him by John, who grabbed his arm and pulled him away.

"Please," John interrupted. "Stop fighting you two. Whatever the woman has done or has not done, she is giving birth in the next chamber and does not need to hear this."

"You are right," James agreed. "But I want Helen out of there."

"Then you best go and get her yourself," Michael replied, knowing his brother would not venture inside the birthing chamber.

"Send a woman in," James demanded.

"No. Christine wants Helen and Helen she shall have."

James sat down on the other end of the settle to his brother and folded his arms, hoping he would not have too long to wait.

"Listen you two," Michael began. "Christine swears Edmund Carstairs abducted her."

"And you believe her?"

"If she is lying, why did John find her back here only a week after she left?"

James shrugged.

"Who knows? Perhaps she realised he was not what she thought he was. Perhaps he did not want to be bothered with a child. He always struck me as a rather immature sort of man."

"I have sent the Constable to question him," Michael told them. "If he abducted her, he should be made to pay."

"It is one way to learn the truth, I suppose."

"I know the truth, James. Carstairs lied to me when he said Christine loved him, he forced her into a position where I would see and think the worst and he abducted her, would have forced himself on her had she not found a way to escape."

"You believe that?" James asked. His eyes met those of John, who shrugged.

"Yes, I believe that," Michael replied. "And I believe something more. I believe I turned my back on the woman I love when she needed me the most. I believe I let her down and left her to her fate, left her at the mercy of a delusional lunatic."

Neither of his brothers spoke, just stared at him doubtfully.

"When you brought her here, John, I was arrogant enough to be thinking about how I would tell her I was willing to forgive her. Now I do not think she will ever forgive me."

CHAPTER TEN

Christine chose a kirtle of cream silk brocade and a surcoat of red velvet to cover it. It was the first day after the birth of her baby son that she had been able to get up and she was anxious to dress, to feel alive again after the months of worry.

Despite the child coming a whole month early and being very small, he was thriving thanks to her insistence on feeding him herself. She had no trust in anyone else; her life had been shattered by the actions of two men, one she had believed a friend, the other she loved.

Now all she wanted was to try to decide the best way forward. Really, it was Michael's decision, but he would never force his opinions or his wishes on her; he was not that manner of husband. After everything she had been through this past summer, she almost wished he was.

Michael made the right noises about accepting the baby, but she still did not believe he meant them. He had come into the chamber after the birth, had sat on the bed and reached into the cradle beside it to stroke the cheek of the sleeping infant.

"It is a boy, Michael," she said. "A son for us, for you."

"A son."

"Yes, a son. Your son. Shall you call him after his father, to tell the world you accept him as your own? Or will you find some excuse to give him a different name?"

"Christine, please. Of course I accept him. Of course he will be Michael."

"And what about the Queen?"

Michael gave her a puzzled frown.

"What about her?"

"You cannot have forgotten her insistence on standing as godmother to your first born son, My Lord."

"I have not forgotten. I will send word to Her Majesty immediately."

His words should have pleased her, but she could not find the sincerity in them she so desperately needed. Now she waited for him to accompany her to the village where she would find Joan, the tenant whose child had missed out on having the Lady of the Manor as his godmother. She would have gone alone, had it not been for Edmund, about whose arrest they had still heard nothing.

She had dressed herself and now she sat and brushed her own long, fair hair. There was an attitude among the servants which made her angry and she feared if she spent time with them, she might dismiss them all and they would have no servants left.

She noticed it first with Lisa's nurse but since then other servants, to whom she had always been able to chat, were very formal. Of course, they all believed she had betrayed their Lord, had run away with her lover, left her baby daughter and broken Lord Melford's heart. Today's visit to the village was not only to apologise to Joan for missing her child's baptism, but to show the tenants and villagers that she had Michael's full support. Whether they would ever believe in her innocence, she could not tell. More likely they would think Michael had forgiven her and taken her back and that in turn would make them think him weak.

The curls were still thick and lustrous, just as they always had been, and she had just replaced the hairbrush on the dresser when she heard raised voices from the chamber next door.

It was Michael's voice and what sounded like that Constable who had come here before the birth, the one she had told to get out as he obviously did not believe a word she said.

"What do you mean, you have not arrested him?" Michael demanded.

"I have no evidence, My Lord," the Constable replied hesitantly. "I questioned him, of course I did. He confirmed that Lady Christine had sent him a note, arranged to meet him at your house."

"Ah, she sent him a note? And did you see this note? Did you confirm it was her own handwriting?"

The Constable shook his head.

"He had burned it," he answered. "She asked him to burn it, lest it be discovered."

Christine was furious. The Constable did not even pretend to doubt it, only accepted Edmund's word as fact. Would Michael also accept it as fact?

"Did he offer any explanation as to why she stayed with him but one night?"

Michael's voice was rising rapidly and as she listened, Christine could not help but feel pleased that at last he was roused to defend her.

"Well, no, My Lord. I am not sure that you should trust her word on that."

Christine caught back a sob. Not only did the Constable think she was lying, he was trying his best to persuade her husband to think the same. Michael's next words would either mend or destroy their marriage and she held her breath as she waited to hear them.

"How dare you? My brother found her in the spring, but I wager you did not even enquire. My wife was right; you had already made up your mind."

"Not at all, My Lord."

"What about his brother? What fairy tale did he tell you about Roger?"

"Lord Roger did die earlier in the year, it is true. But he died of food poisoning, as Her Ladyship was told. One of the servants who finished his meal suffered the same fate."

Michael laughed derisively.

"And does that not cause you suspicion?"

"I am sorry, My Lord, I could find no evidence against Mr Carstairs."

"You know what?" Michael said. "It was obvious to me that you did not believe a word of my wife's statement when she gave it. Little wonder she was reluctant to report the abduction; she likely expected this. I do not believe you even attempted to properly examine the accused. Get out of my sight!"

Christine peered through the crack where the hinges held the door open and saw the Constable hand some scrolls to Michael, who frowned suspiciously.

"What is this?"

"It is a transcript of my interview with Mr Carstairs," the Constable replied. "You might want to consider using it to bring your own charges."

"Against Carstairs?"

"Well, My Lord. Mr Carstairs assured me Her Ladyship was a willing party, that she asked him to meet her. You might well be successful in bringing a charge of adultery against them both."

The crash which followed the Constable's words sent Christine into the next chamber to see the man sprawled out on the floor, clutching his bleeding mouth and lying against an overturned settle.

"Michael," she said, gripping his arm before he had a chance to hit the man again. "Have a care. He is the Constable."

"Constable?" Michael spat. "He is as useless as a posy to ward off plague! Do you know what he suggested?"

"Yes, I heard."

The Constable struggled to his feet and quickly backed away towards the door.

"Get out!" Michael yelled at him. "Leave my house and do not return. And if you dare spread your lies about the county, I will know where to come for revenge."

Christine clung to Michael's arm as they stood and watched the Constable leave and he turned his head and gave her that warm smile which could always melt her heart.

"Did you mean it?" She said. "Or were you simply trying to save face?"

He pulled her into his arms and kissed her lips, a long, passionate kiss that made her feel that she would meld with him, would lose herself altogether. God, how she had missed that! She snuggled her head against him, felt the warmth from his chest where his shirt fell open, and wrapped her arms around him.

The memories she had suppressed since her return, the ones she had buried beneath pride and anger, came flooding back and she needed Michael to understand just what she had suffered, just what he had put her through by being too kind, by not fighting for her.

"Michael, I was so frightened," she said. "When I told Edmund I would not share his bed, he got angry. I had to be nice to him, I had to pretend I really wanted him to persuade him to wait. I had to climb out of the window and walk back here through the forest; it is a frightening place, the forest. All those trees making it dark, all those strange noises. There could have been wolves in there and I was afraid of getting lost."

"My poor darling," Michael murmured. "I am so sorry."

"And all the time I was afraid he would find me, that he would leap out from behind a tree and grab me." She was sobbing now, soaking his linen shirt till it clung to his flesh. "It took me all day to get here, all day and when I arrived, thinking that at last I could rest, at last I could eat, there he was, waiting for me."

"Christine, if I could take it back..."

"I had to rest; I was so tired and I was scared of losing the babe from all the trauma. My feet were soaked and bruised where I had trodden on stones and brambles. I know not what made me think of the old fisherman's cottage. I was not even sure if it was still standing, but I slept there for over a week, waiting for the family to return. And every night I fought against sleep, too scared to relax lest Edmund came whilst I slept."

"What can I say?"

"And the more scared I was, the more wretched I was, the more I resented you for leaving me with him. I am not sure if that feeling will ever go away."

***

Christine's words pounded in Michael's mind as he rode beside her to the village. He could not believe he had made such a terrible mistake, caused her so much suffering and abandoned her to be assaulted by a lunatic.

James was right; he was weak. How else could this have happened? He might have lost her forever because of that weakness, and it seemed all the law could do was to side with the perpetrator of the crime.

People stopped what they were doing and stared as Lord and Lady Melford rode slowly into the village, just as they always had, but this time was different. This time there were no smiles of greeting, no friendly waves, only long faces with condemnation in their eyes.

They dismounted and left the horses tied to a rail, then went to the little square cottage which was the home of Joan.

She looked up from the baby and jumped to her feet, curtseying quickly.

"My Lord," she said, then turned her eyes to Christine before her voice and eyes dropped. "My Lady."

"Joan," Christine said at once. "I have come to offer my regrets at not being able to stand as godmother to your son, as I promised."

Joan's gaze remained fixed on the dirt floor.

"I heard, My Lady," she said. "That you were otherwise engaged."

Christine caught back a sob and turned to run out of the cottage, but Michael stopped her, put his arms around her and turned back to the peasant woman.

"Mistress Joan," he said. "Lady Christine has been through a terrible ordeal. She came back here in the spring to fulfil her promise to you, but she was abducted by a man who dragged her away, imprisoned her and threatened to rape her. That is how she was otherwise engaged."

Joan's eyes grew round as they stared back at him, then moved to where Christine stood, leaning against him for support.

"My Lady?" She said. "Forgive me. We were all told something quite different."

"Yes," Christine spat angrily. "Everyone will believe that, will they not? Even my husband believed that, people who should have known better. How am I ever going live with that? I suppose you think me unworthy to be godmother to your future babes?"

"No, My Lady." Joan took a step forward and gripped Christine's arm. "Forgive me, My Lady, but I fear I might have been the cause of your distress."

Christine turned puzzled eyes on her.

"How so?"

"A man came to the village, just as my husband and the other villagers were getting things ready for our baptism, and he asked what was going on. I told him we were expecting Lady Melford to come and be godmother." She paused and bit her lip. "Please tell me it was not the man who abused you."

Christine wished she could, but the confession only made matters worse.

"Michael, can we go home now, please," she said. "Coming here was not a good idea. Showing my face anywhere is not a good idea. Everywhere I go they think I am a harlot."

"No, sweetheart, we will make them see."

"Will we? I am a harlot and my husband is weak to take me back, to forgive me. I am sullied, unclean, soiled. Yet I did nothing! Nothing! It is so unfair!"

CHAPTER ELEVEN

Michael made the decision when he returned to Melford Hall with his wife. After seeing the reaction of the villagers to her, after making a feeble effort to comfort her sobs, he knew what he had to do. If the Constable would not arrest Edmund, would not lock him up in prison to keep Christine safe, Michael would have to deal with him himself.

Not only was the man allowed to get away with murdering his own brother and abducting Michael's wife, he was also a continuing threat to her. She was not able to go anywhere without a guard of some sort to protect her, lest Edmund Carstairs be lurking, waiting for his opportunity to snatch her away again.

He went to the nursery, picked up his little daughter and kissed her, then moved to study the tiny baby boy who lie in his crib, a little stronger now, but still in need of extra care. As Michael gazed at him, a tremor of regret touched his heart. Christine was right; he had looked at this little scrap of humanity when he was first born and had not believed he was his son, not really. He had felt no love for him, unlike the feeling he had for Lisa when she was born; he felt only doubt. Now he looked down at the sleeping babe and that love began to surge, began to fill his heart. Yes, the boy was his and his wife loved him, had always loved him. How could he have ever thought otherwise?

There was but one way to make it up to her, one way to prove to her how much she meant to him.

Michael knew he had been a complete fool, had allowed his jealousy to take her away from him. As he thought about the time since their marriage, he remembered what he should have remembered all along. He recalled her sweet love, the way she would greet him with a kiss, the way she would turn and kiss his nipple as they lie in bed after making love, the way she would run her lips over his body until he shivered with desire.

No woman could pretend those things, not a woman like Christine anyway. Perhaps a prostitute might have such skills, but a woman like his wife would only do those things out of love. And he had been too stupid to see it.

And the child, his baby son, and he was his son, nobody else's. Michael knew that now, but was it too late? Would she ever forgive him? That little baby was the heir to the Melford estate, he was the godchild of Queen Elizabeth and favoured with great gifts from her.

And this babe's father very nearly lost it all; he might still have lost it all if Christine could not forgive him. Would he ever convince his brothers of the truth? He thought John would be easily persuaded, but what of James?

Whatever happened, he had no intention of allowing Edmund Carstairs to remain at large, free to threaten Christine's safety a second time.

***

It was nearly noon when Michael arrived at Carstairs Manor. The house was small compared to Melford Hall and even to the Manor House, but it was comfortable enough. He had been here once before, when Edmund's father lived, but he remembered very little about the place. He could not even recall precisely why he had been there, but he seemed to remember accompanying Malcolm to some function or other.

He had considered telling Christine of his intention to come here, but he realised his only reason for doing so was to make her see that he was on her side. That would only worry her and it was selfish. He told John though; it was safer for someone to know where he had gone and he was still not on speaking terms with James.

"Then I am coming with you," John had said.

"No. I need to do this alone."

"If what you say is true, that he abducted and threatened your wife, he is deranged. You should not face him alone."

"Perhaps not, but it is what I have to do. I let her down, John! Do you not see that? I could never live with myself if I did not make certain Carstairs can never hurt her again, and I need to do it alone."

"What are you planning, Michael?"

"I am planning to confront him. I am planning on making him fight for her, as I should have fought for her. Perhaps I can force him to sign a confession."

"And what will she think if you are killed? You have no way of knowing what sort of swordsman he is."

"That is true," Michael answered thoughtfully. "But it is logical that a man who would intimidate a woman as he did, would be a coward. I am only telling you my intentions in case I do not return, so you will know where to look. Give me until this evening, then you can come after me."

"But, Michael, I can help."

"No. Stay here, look after Christine. Please."

"It seems that has been my role in life in recent months," John answered as he turned away. "Looking after Christine."

Michael looked at him sharply, his frown one of disapproval.

"I am sorry," John muttered. "That was uncalled for. If you are sure she is innocent, I will believe her, and I will look after her. Just please be careful; I do not want to have to look after her forever."

It was about an hour later that Helen arrived, angrily followed by James who strode into the house, calling out to his wife.

"Helen!" He shouted. "I am telling you for the last time. You will not visit that woman."

Helen stopped and turned to face him, making John wonder if he would have to intervene. Neither of them had noticed him seated in the great hall, but he was used to that. Remembering James' threats towards Christine, he was prepared to defend Helen if necessary.

"James," Helen said facing him. "Christine is my friend. She has few friends now, thanks to you and your brother and your accusations without proof. She needs me and I want to see the baby."

"Christine is a whore," James retorted. "I do not want you anywhere near her."

"Even if that were true, James, it is not contagious. Christine did nothing; she was an innocent, faithful wife who had the misfortune to be the obsession of a madman. If you cannot see how much she loves your brother, you deserve no say in the matter."

"Helen!"

She turned and carried on towards Christine's bedchamber while James stopped and watched her go and John grinned, amused by the entire scene. He had never seen this before; always

Helen was very obedient to her husband's wishes, very respectful, but it seemed that she would only obey him when she agreed with him and in this case she did not.

Good! It would be good for James to realise he was not in charge after all.

"Where is Michael?" He demanded.

John did not answer straight away. He was not sure if Michael really wanted James to know where he had gone, but eventually he thought he would have to tell him or he would not give up.

"He has gone to have it out with Edmund Carstairs," he answered.

"What? He will get himself killed."

"I do not think so," John replied. "Michael is a competent swordsman; in fact, I would say he is an exceptional swordsman. The Constable can find no evidence to arrest the man and Michael feels it his duty to make sure he is no longer in a position to harm Christine."

James opened his mouth to reply when soft laughter was heard from the gallery as the two women began to descend the stairs together. James spun around, still angry that his wife had defied him so publicly, and now furious with Christine for putting Michael in danger.

He took a threatening step towards the stairs and both women stopped.

"Now, see what you have achieved!" James shouted. "You wanted him to fight for you and it seems you have your wish."

"What are you talking about?"

"Oh, yes, pretend you do not know that my brother has gone to see Carstairs."

Christine only stared at him, then her eyes moved to rest on John.

"It is true, Christine," he said. "He said he cannot allow him to be free to try again."

"No."

Christine was shaking her head, a look of terror in her eyes.

"If my brother is killed," James told her, "I will know who to blame. And do not imagine your bastard will be the next earl, either. I will have that title and I will make sure you are both thrown out of here at the first opportunity."

"No, James!" Helen said as she lifted her skirts and ran down the stairs to face her husband. "Christine has done nothing."

"So you say."

"It is true, James," Christine said. "I love Michael; I have always loved Michael and I would never have betrayed him. A man I thought was a friend lied to him, told him his delusional ideas, and he believed him. You all believed him, all except Helen and Grace. They knew better, even a young maid like Grace knew better than you educated gentlemen."

James exchanged a glance with his younger brother, who shrugged.

"Is this true?"

"Of course it is true," Christine replied. "If I was going to run away with Edmund Carstairs, I would have done it before my marriage, not waited until I had a child and a man who would be hurt by it. But I care nothing for your opinion, only Michael's. And you must go after him. You must stop him!"

***

Michael dismounted and tied his horse to a tree before approaching the house on foot. He wanted to use stealth, did not want Carstairs to see him coming and if what Christine told him was true, and he was certain now that it was, the man could easily ambush him if given warning of his approach.

Michael reminded himself that he was dealing with a madman, a man who would not accept that the woman he had set his sights on did not want him, had never wanted him.

He crept close to the house and peered through the window to see Edmund Carstairs seated beside the fireplace with a goblet in his hand. He was slouched in his chair, staring at the hearth, which held no fire, and he looked thoughtful. Michael wondered what he was scheming in his deranged mind, wondered if he was making plans to return to Melford Hall and make another attempt to take Michael's wife away from him.

The idea pinched his heart and he realised with a jolt that he was no longer jealous, only angry. He stared at Carstairs for a little while and as he stared he recalled all the glorious nights of passion he had spent with his wife, all the endearments, the joy in her eyes and her manner when she saw him, and he wondered why he could not have remembered all those things before.

No, he was no longer jealous. Now he knew that Christine had no love for this man, that her heart belonged to her husband and her husband was a bloody fool who did not deserve that heart.

He moved to the front door, clasping the hilt of his sword where it rested in its scabbard as he did so. He tried the door handle and was relieved to find it opened easily. He stepped inside the house and was assailed by the smell of putrid food in the air. A quick glance round told him Carstairs had no servants; the place was filthy, looked as though it had not been cleaned in months.

On the table were the rotting remains of a banquet and Michael recalled Christine telling him about the feast Edmund had prepared for her. Could this really be the same food as he had laid out months ago to welcome what he thought of as his lady love? Judging by the state of it and the fetid stench which wafted from it, it seemed likely. The fruit was almost liquid where it had rotted away, the meat was covered in furry mould and rats scuttled between the filthy dishes, proving that even the rats would not eat it. The flies were not so particular though and they covered the table. Michael did not get close enough to see the fat maggots they would have left in their wake, but he could well imagine them.

Michael moved closer to the man sitting before the hearth, noticed the cobwebs hanging in the corners, noticed a black rat scuttling across the floor near Carstairs' foot, but still the man sat and stared into the cold grate.

"Mr Carstairs," Michael said.

Edmund's eyes moved up to look at Michael and he smiled.

"Lord Melford," he replied. He put his goblet down on the hearthstone and got to his feet. "You have come about Lady Christine? You have finally realised that she loves me, and will never be happy with you."

Michael's fury rose up, threatened to overtake common sense.

"I came to tell you to leave her alone," he said. "But obviously you have still not accepted that she loves me. I was a jealous fool to let her go, but the fact that she ran away should tell you she wants to be with me."

"She ran away because she wanted to protect me," he said. "She was afraid you would come after us and harm me, harm her as well."

Michael wanted to argue, but he knew it was pointless and the more this man said, the angrier he became. His grip tightened around the hilt of his sword.

"You lied to the Constable. You care nothing for her reputation, for the way she is treated by the people on the estate, for the opinion of her peers. How can you pretend to love her?"

"None of that matters," he said. "The only thing that matters is that she is with me, where she belongs."

"How can you even think that?"

"Before you came along and stole her away, we had something special. I would visit her every day at the Duke's estate and she always welcomed me. Then you came and made her believe she loved you, not me."

"She was right; you are mad."

"She will be back," Edmund said. "I heard she had another child, a child who came too early. Now I know why she ran away, why she wanted to wait. She could not be with me while she carried your brat, could she? She is far too much of a lady to do that."

Michael only stared at him, his mind crowded with memories of the birth of his son, of how he doubted the boy's parentage. Christine had told him; why did it take the enemy's word to finally convince him?

"Once she has made sure the babe will survive, then she will return to me. You will see, Lord Melford, that you cannot buy your way into the lives of others."

"And you cannot force your way in. I let Christine go because I thought that was what she wanted, because I loved her that much. You only want to own her; you would force her away from her children, her husband. That is not love."

"I killed my brother to be with Christine," Edmund said, then he turned and grabbed a sword which was lying on the chest. "I shall have no hesitation in doing the same to you."

Then he thrust the blade toward Michael who backed out of the house while drawing his own sword from its scabbard. He wanted to be outside, where there was room to manoeuvre. He would have little chance to overcome Carstairs inside the house and he had no idea what sort of swordsman he was facing.

Edmund came out into the yard, still thrusting his sword towards Michael, who easily leapt out of the way. Edmund thrust again, but he was no match for Michael whose father had insisted all his sons be highly trained in the art of fencing, lest they be called upon to defend the realm.

Edmund's body resisted Michael's blade as it plunged into him and he doubled up as the sword was withdrawn. He clutched at his midriff, blood pouring over his hands, his eyes full of hatred as he stared into the last face he would ever see on this earth.

"Tell Christine I love her," he whispered hoarsely as he fell to the ground.

***

Michael's two brothers arrived at Carstairs Manor just an hour after Michael himself, while Edmund Carstairs' life force was draining into the sandy earth of the yard. Michael sat beside him, watched the light go out of his eyes, watched all colour drain away and felt relieved. He would never have to worry about this man taking his wife; she would be able to live her life without the constant threat of being abducted again.

But he also felt relieved to have confirmation that little Michael was entitled to wear that name and with that relief came tremendous guilt. He should never have doubted her, not for one moment. Was it too much to expect forgiveness for that? He thought it best if she never knew, but he knew it was too late for that. She knew him too well, she knew how he had felt.

He stared down at the stiffening body on the ground at his feet and he wanted to kill it all over again. He had never known such hatred before.

Since he met Christine he had learned about love, but he had also learned about anger, jealousy and now hatred. He also knew about shame, shame that he had ever doubted her, that he had ever given Edmund Carstairs the ability to ruin their lives.

He stood up when he heard the horses, glanced up at his brothers and smiled bitterly.

"It is over," James said as he approached Michael.

"Is it? It seems to me I have a lot of repairs to make."

"So have I," James replied. "I am sorry, Michael. I said some terrible things to you, both to you and to Christine."

Michael stared at him, his eyes narrowing.

"You believe her now? Why?"

"I am not sure I believe her, but it is not my business, as John said."

Michael shook his head then went to mount his own horse.

"I will go to the Justice of the Peace, tell him what has happened here."

"No," John said. "I will go. You need to go home to your wife. She is frantic with worry."

"Ah, but is she frantic with worry about Michael, or about Carstairs?" James remarked. "Michael, it is up to you whether you take her back, but for all you know she was no maid when you married her."

Michael laughed, as though he had heard something really funny.

"Sometimes, James, I wonder what world you live in," he said, looking down from his tall horse, the horse he had bought at the same time as he had bought Christine. "A man can tell if a woman is a maid, surely you know that."

James made no reply, but he frowned thoughtfully.

"I will stay here until John returns with the Justice," he muttered, then went inside the house to find a chair.

***

Christine sat on the steps outside the main doors of the Melford Hall, her arms folded to keep out the autumn chill, and waited. She sat in the very same place where Edmund had sat, where she had seen him when she finally arrived, exhausted, having walked through the damp forest to get here.

Helen tried to coax her back inside, but she refused to go and at last she had given up trying to persuade her and brought her a warm cloak.

She had been there for hours, just waiting for news, waiting to see if she had gone from being a betrayed wife to a widow, with no respite in between.

She prayed as she waited, prayed for the safety of the man she loved and she promised God that if he would only bring Michael home safely, she would put this year behind them and give herself up to loving her husband. Is that not what God wanted? She had taken those vows in that little church and she had no right to break them, just because she was disappointed. And she did so long to hold Michael in her arms again, so yearned to feel his body against her again.

She had no way of knowing whether Edmund was an accomplished swordsman, but she knew her husband was. He had told her his father had insisted on all his sons learning the skills of swordsmanship and they all kept up the practice, in case it was ever needed.

Well, now it was needed and she hated knowing that. Even if Edmund was not the swordsman Michael was, Michael could still be ambushed before he had a chance to see the man. He could be killed and if he was, Christine swore she would have revenge on Edmund Carstairs. He would know once and for all how she felt about him.

At last she heard the horse approach, just one horse. Where were the others? She raised her eyes fearfully, afraid of what she would see, of who she would see. Would it be John, come alone to break bad news? Or would it be James, spitting more hateful accusations at her?

She leapt to her feet when she saw the huge, black stallion trotting towards her, and she let go of all the tears to which she had been holding fast. The relief was indescribable. As Michael dismounted, a stable boy ran to take the horse's reins and lead him away.

"See to him immediately," Michael told the boy. "He has had a long journey and he deserves the best care."

Then he turned towards the house and strode quickly to meet his wife as she ran into his arms.

"Michael," she cried. "I was so frightened. Why did you not tell me where you were going?"

"Because there was no need for you to know. I had to do it, Christine. I should have done this in the beginning, the first time he came here. I should have given you the respect you deserve and asked you for the truth, instead of believing what he said. I am such a fool. Will you ever forgive me?"

"Edmund?" She asked.

His eyes met hers and held her gaze. Would she be sad to learn of Carstairs' death? Would she blame Michael for killing him, or would she be happy that her safety is secure?

"I killed him," he answered at last, then added hastily: "It was self defence, he came after me first."

He had to assure her of that. Somehow he thought she would not approve of his killing

Carstairs in cold blood, no matter what threat he posed. His heart sang when she breathed a sigh of relief and reached up to kiss his lips, to kiss him with the passion he had not known since he let her go.

"We are safe?" she said. "We will never see him again?"

"We are safe, but can we get back what he stole away? Can you forgive me for not respecting you enough, for not knowing he was lying? What can I do to make it up to you?"

She kissed him again.

"You can come to bed and show me how much you love me," she said. "That is what you can do."

THE END

Author's Note: Thank you for reading The Elizabethans: The Earl's Jealousy. I hope you have enjoyed it and if you have, please leave a review on the Amazon website.

Book Two in the series, The Viscount's Pride, is available now.

If you would like advance notification of when this book is released, please join my Readers' Group (information on my website at http://www.historical-romance.com). You will also receive some free books when you join.

Please consider my other books:

Holy Poison is a series of six books which follow the lives of ordinary people who lived through the reign of Queen Mary I, also known as Bloody Mary for her violent campaign to return England to the Catholic Church of Rome.

Book 1: The Judas Pledge
Book 2: The Flawed Mistress
Book 3: The Viscount's Birthright

Book 4: Betrayal
Book 5: The Heretics
Book 6: Consequences

Also available as a boxed set

Praise for Holy Poison:

"The 6 books of holy poison are among some of the best books I have read, I could not put them down and the last one had me crying, What an author. I would have given it 10 stars if I could."

More historical romance/fiction:

The Wronged Wife
The Scent of Roses
The Gorston Widow
A Man in Mourning
The Adulteress
The Crusader's Widow
To Catch a Demon
The Romany Princess

Mystery/thriller:

Mirielle
Old Fashioned Values

Your Free Books

When you join our readers' group you will receive these books absolutely free, two of which are on sale for $3.99 each. The third one is exclusive to our group.

What Else? As well as these three books you will receive:

Advance notification of special offers, advance chapters of new releases and free access to all new books and materials which are exclusive to members.

All you have to do to join is Tell me where to send your FREE books – **go to my website www.historical-romance.com**

Your email address will never be shared and you can leave the group at any time.

The Final Confession of Richard Summerville – Members' Only Exclusive

This confession was written by Lord Richard Summerville, of the Holy Poison series, just before his death in 1578. He hid it away, as it was written to ease his conscience, not for the eyes of others. But it was found in 1917, when the War Office took over Summerville Hall to use as a hospital for wounded soldiers.

It is not on sale to the general public, nor will it be - it is available now only to members of our historical romance readers' group.

***

A Medieval Romance - It is 1139 and the Empress Maud has landed in England to lay claim to the English throne, currently occupied by her cousin Stephen. David, Lord Ravenscroft is a chief advisor to King Stephen and is away at court, helping to plan a strategy to defeat the Empress. His world collapses when, during a search for the Empress which includes his own house, a naked man is discovered in his wife's bed. She can offer no explanation other than the obvious one, that she has a lover. David leaves, never to return, until he receives word from Catherine that she is dying and needs to tell him the truth.

This is a tale of one woman's sacrifice to protect the men she loves, during the nineteen year Anarchy, one of England's many civil wars.

***

After waiting impatiently for the return of her husband, Philip, from the third crusade in the Holy Land, Lady Isabella Whyford is devastated when his cousin, Roger, returns alone and with the news that Philip is dead. As his heir, Roger begins to lay claim to the estate but he intends to lay claim to Isabella as well. When she refuses, he seeks the help of Prince John who commands the marriage. When Isabella discovers what Roger has promised the Prince in return, she has no option but to flee.

CPSIA information can be obtained at www.ICGtesting.com
Printed in the USA
LVOW06s1914271215

468000LV00023B/1001/P